DEMIGODS ACADEMY

THE CAVE OF MEMORY

BOOK
5

CHAPTER ONE

MELANY

"Hello?" I called into the great void, my voice bouncing back to me as if I was in a cave.

Yet, I knew that wasn't where I was. Caves had walls, and ceilings, and floors. There was definitely none of that around me. At least not on my first inspection, where I blindly reached out a hand in front of me, beside me, and above me. I was literally standing in a gray misty arena of nothingness. Even the very air had no substance to it.

Turning around, I squinted into the fog gently floating all around, trying to make out something, anything nearby, but I couldn't spy any shape in any direction. I swiped a hand through the mist, watching it swirl around then settle back into its original space.

It was odd. Mist usually didn't behave like that, like a living, breathing, thinking entity.

My feet carefully moved forward, and I reached out a hand again, hoping that after each step I took I would eventually touch something solid—like the rough edge of stone, or even a tree. So far, all I'd been able to grab was handfuls of inert fog. After another step, I crouched and felt the ground beneath me. Once more, all I came away with was mist, not rock, or grass, or anything of substance. I swallowed as my stomach roiled, realizing I wasn't walking on anything, which seemed impossible. I wasn't floating. At least I didn't think I was.

Standing, I whirled around in a circle. "Hello?!" Nothing but my own panicked voice bounced back to my ears. Obviously, Nyx, the Goddess of the Night, had been true to her word.

She had snapped me into oblivion.

What that truly meant, I had no idea. All I knew was that I wasn't in the Temple of Night any longer, and it seemed I wasn't really anywhere. I still existed, thank the Gods. I pinched my own arm to

DEMIGODS ACADEMY

THE CAVE OF MEMORY

ELISA S. AMORE

KIERA LEGEND

make sure I was still corporeal. I was, and the pinch hurt.

I could still feel pain. I could still feel my heart thundering inside my chest. I could hear the rush of blood in my ears, as I tried to fight back the panic that threatened to explode inside my head. Some things still existed, like me, but I was afraid I might be the only thing that did in this place.

Once I decided that the best thing to do, the most logical, was to keep moving around, I hoped to run into something. Anything at all. At that point, I didn't really care what that something was. I'd gladly run into a pit of snakes, or even fall off the edge of a cliff. It would at least be evidence of some kind of reality.

After every five steps I took, I stopped, splayed my arms and swished them back and forth, hoping to touch something. I never did. It was just gray mist all around me, in every direction. I wasn't sure how long I walked. All sense of time had vanished from my mind. It could've been hours, or minutes, I wasn't certain. The only indication that some time had passed was the aching of my leg muscles from exertion.

Ceasing my attempts, I sat to rub my legs. It was as much for comfort as I did to ease my nerves.

What if this was it for me? What if I was lost for all eternity, doomed to do nothing but walk aimlessly around some empty world? Would I starve to death because there was no food or water? Would I go completely mad and rip open the veins in my arms to end my suffering? I hated that I was already thinking about that, and I'd only just been sent here.

Frowning, I massaged one ankle then the other, relieving the tightness. I *had* only just arrived here, right? Hours ago, I'd been talking with Thanatos in the garden right outside Nyx's sky temple. No, it had been minutes. Wait. Maybe it had been a day or two.

Curious to know if I was hungry, I rubbed a hand over my stomach. I didn't feel hungry, so it couldn't have been days. It had to have been only an hour or two ago. I rubbed my hands over my face in frustration.

Gods! I was already going nuts questioning myself over and over again. I had to get the hell out of here.

I should've listened to Tisiphone and left with her, but no, I had to do things my way. As usual. And as usual, it got me into trouble. Would she tell people where I was if they came looking for me? I wasn't sure she would, she was that petty.

After getting to my feet, I unfurled my wings. Flying around would be a better way to figure out where I was. Stretching them out as far as they would go, I flapped them once, twice more to lift into the air, but it didn't work, or at least it didn't feel like it worked. Maybe it had, and I was floating and didn't know it because I couldn't really feel the ground beneath me, or see it. Everything looked as lifeless and gray as before. There had been no change.

Hands fisting, I pressed them hard against my legs, and screamed.

I waited, straining to hear any sound to be returned. At first all I could hear was my own heartbeat, thudding along my pulse points in my throat, and the sound of every ragged breath of air I took. Then I started to make out another sound underneath that self-contained noise in my ears. It sounded like water rushing.

Excited for the first sign of life in this desolate emptiness, I took a few steps forward, stopped, and listened for the sound again. It seemed to be getting louder, so I moved forward a little more, then stopped. Straining to hear, I searched. Maybe the rushing was getting quieter, so I adjusted my direction, and took a few steps again until the sound got louder.

For what seemed like hours, I did that—shuffle a few steps, stop and listen—although time didn't really exist there, I didn't think. Maybe it moved differently, or not at all. I didn't know, and thinking about it, hurt my head, so I tried not to think about it too much.

However long it took me, eventually, the rushing of water became loud, echoing all around me. It was like being on the edge of the River Styx as the black water surged by, or at the bottom of a tall waterfall with its cascade pounding on the rocks. I figured soon I would see it. At least I hoped I'd see it before I fell into it.

After another few steps, I could feel something in the air. When I thrust my hand out in front of me, I felt the moisture on the tips of my fingers and palm. Smiling at my discovery, I took a big stride, and almost went head first into what appeared to be —if I squinted hard enough—a lively river. Pulling my leg back, I sunk to my knees on the bank, thankful that there was actual solidness beneath me.

I peered at the river. At first it was only just a darker gray smudge on the ground, but after looking at it long enough, more details started to emerge. Like the small pebbles along the shore, and the bigger rocks jutting out from the water. A few plants, a very muted green color, sprouted along the bank. Lifting my head, more shapes and forms came into focus, as if by magic. It was as if my eyes could finally *see*.

Standing tall, on the opposite side of the riverbank from where I knelt, a grouping of trees appeared. I couldn't tell what kind they were—maybe oak, based on how big and wide they were. Downstream, along the shore, I spotted an outcropping of big rocks, with more smaller plants dotting the ground.

I breathed a huge sigh of relief. Obviously, I wasn't in a place of complete nothingness. There was life here. It was just shrouded in a bleak desolate fog. Patting the ground I knelt on, I felt dirt and bits of rock under my fingers. It was solid beneath me, not like before where I seemed to be walking on the mist itself. Comforted by seeing and feeling these things around me, I almost laughed.

At least, I knew I'd been sent somewhere. If it was a place that existed, I figured it was a place I could get out of. There was always a way. I had learned that over the past couple of years at the academy.

If I followed the river, I wondered where it would lead me. Maybe nowhere, but it was a starting point, and I wouldn't be any less off than I already was. The greater the risk, the greater the reward, right?

Hell, right now, I'd be satisfied with just not being left to die in this gray void.

Since there were trees and water, then there had to be sustenance; at least I wouldn't starve. There had to be food somewhere. I might have to eat bugs and leaves, but it would be something. As I thought about it, my stomach suddenly woke up and started to rumble. My mouth and throat went dry.

Frigid cold washed against my skin and a shiver rushed up my arms and along my back. My mouth felt like sandpaper, so I cupped some water between my palms and brought it to my lips.

"Don't drink it!"

With the warning, I was shoved to the side, the liquid spilling from my fingers to be absorbed by the dirt.

"Drinking it will make you lose your memories. You'll forget who you are and why you're here. And you'll never want to leave."

Blinking in shock, I looked up toward the dark shape hovering over me. She had long black hair, scraggily and tangled around a pale triangular face. Her dress, also black, was equally a mess, torn here and there as if she'd been in a terrible fight. The hem that surrounded her pale, bare feet was in tatters.

The last time I'd seen her was on the eve of the big battle against the Titans and Zeus. She'd come to Hades's Hall to fight on our side.

"Hecate?" I choked out the words. "How did you end up here?"

"The same way I suspect that you are here." She swiped at the dark hair hanging in her eyes. "I angered the wrong person."

CHAPTER TWO

MELANY

I got to my feet, feeling uncomfortable with the witch goddess looming over me. I'd heard about her unpredictability, and the different "sides" to her personality, so I didn't want to be taken by surprise. Especially not now, when I felt like I was standing on uneven ground.

"What is this place?" I asked.

"Asphodel Meadows," she explained. "It's a place between life and death."

"How long have you been here?"

Hecate swiped at her hair again, then worried

on her bottom lip. "I'm not sure." She eyed me. "When did I see you last?"

"Around four months ago, at the battle in Pecunia." I gaped at her. "You've been here that long?"

"Maybe?" She flinched and scratched at her ear just under her hair. "After the battle, I remember going back to my tree and seeing that it had been destroyed. I didn't have any other place to go." She scratched again, her shoulder twitched. "A friend offered me a place to stay, but his mother didn't like it very much."

With a humorless chuckle, I shook my head. "Let me guess? That mother happened to be Nyx, the Goddess of the Night?"

"Yes." Her eyes widened. "I can assume she also sent you here with a snap of her bony fingers."

I nodded. "Yup, she's a bitch of the first order."

Hecate's lips twitched up a bit at that. "I concur."

"Have you been alone this whole time?"

She nodded, and her shoulder twitched again.

I didn't know Hecate well, only heard dubious stories about her from other people, including Lucian, who had given her his blood for passage to the underworld to save me, but I was glad to have someone else to rely on in this place. I couldn't imagine being totally alone, especially not for as long as Hecate had been here. I had a sense that it had affected her. She seemed a bit twitchy, but I supposed I would be too if I hadn't anyone to talk to for months.

"Since we can't drink the water from the river, where have you been drinking from? Oh, and food. Where can I get some?" My stomach growled again, reminding me I hadn't eaten in some time.

Hecate grabbed my arm. "Come. I will show you."

I followed her along the riverbank, close enough that I could see her, but not so close that I stepped on the backs of her heels. We passed the grouping of large rocks that I spied earlier, then she veered off to the left. After another maybe twenty feet, something large loomed ahead. I couldn't quite make it out, it was all just a dark gray, muddled blur in front of me—just as the river had been before I'd nearly fell into it.

Eventually that blur sharpened, and I could see that it was a large hill. Not a mountain, or cliffs like there had been in Elysium, but just a really big rolling hill. In that hill was an entrance to a cave dug out of the dirt and rock. Hecate led me inside.

Nothing but pitch black greeted us once we

entered, and I wondered if the goddess, being so close to the darkness, could actually see. I on the other hand, could not. So, I cupped my hands together and formed a small ball of fire to light the way. The flames were muted, like everything else in this place, but they produced enough light that I didn't automatically bump into the walls.

The cave wasn't deep, more of a cut-out than anything else, so it didn't take long before Hecate stopped to show me how she'd been surviving. In it was a small pool of water—probably run off from somewhere—and I spied a pile of what looked like berries, a few mushrooms, and a spit made from twigs constructed over a small fire pit contained by stones. On it, there was also the remnants of some kind of cooked rodent, I assumed.

Seeing her setup made my stomach roil. The thought of living here for an eternity—eating sour berries and roasting whatever that was leftover on the spit—made me want to retch. I refused to do that. That wouldn't be my fate. No freaking way.

She gestured to the pool of water. "It's good and clean. Won't take your memories."

Crouching near it, I cupped the cool liquid into my hands and brought them to my mouth, but hesitated for a moment. Could I truly trust her? Hecate remembered me, so that had to be proof she wasn't lying. I sipped the water, instantly quenching my thirst, and then I drank more.

Afterward, I sat there and pulled up memory after memory of my life in the academy to make sure I still had them. Images of Lucian popped into my mind, as well as my friends Georgina and Jasmine. Like usual, thoughts and memories of Hades filled me to the brim until I felt like I was going to explode.

I got to my feet and rubbed at my face, hoping to scrub them away, at least for a bit so I could think and figure out a way to get out of here and back to the land of the living.

"Have you tried to get out of here?"

Hecate turned her head toward me, but her lips didn't move when I heard a gravely voice berate me. "Of course we have, you disrespectful little bimbo."

Bimbo? That was the first time I'd ever been called that. Frowning, I eyed her. "Did you just call me a bimbo?"

Her whole body shook, and twitched, then her head turned to the side in a sickening twist, until a different face scowled at me. This one was old and haggard, with rheumy eyes, a crooked nose, and liver spots all over her sallow cheeks. When she snarled at me, she revealed rotten brown teeth.

"Would you prefer I call you hussy, jezebel, or tramp?"

"How about you don't call me any of those things? My name is Melany. You can use my name, thank you very much."

She waved a dismissive hand at me. "Then don't ask a stupid question, girl."

Her body shook and convulsed again, her head turning back to its original position. Hecate swiped at her hair. "Sorry about that. Yes, I tried following the river, but it seemed to go in a circle. I climbed on top of this hill to scout out the rest of the meadows, but as you've by now noticed, this gray mist shrouds everything. You can't see anything until you are almost upon it."

"Have you used your magic?"

She nodded. "I've conjured everything I could think of, but nothing worked. Everything is muted here even my magic."

I'd noticed that earlier when I formed a fire ball, and wondered if it would be like that with all my other powers. I guessed the best thing for me to do was to try, although, I wasn't quite sure how to use them to escape this place. The most logical one to try first would be my shadow power. That one had a greater chance to getting us somewhere else.

For the optimum possibility, I decided to stay in the cave as it produced more darkness. I expanded the light source by building onto my fire ball, though it was hard to create more flames. The air felt oppressive and heavy. Eventually, I grew the ball to the size of a basketball, and settled it in the center of the cave.

Shadows formed in every corner, and I reached for them. At first, they wouldn't obey me, stubbornly staying in place. I had to concentrate harder on them, calling to them to form around me. In the end, I was able to draw a few of them forward and I caped myself with them, reveling in the familiar feel of darkness. I breathed them in, and it was like taking in oxygen after being deprived for a long time.

Grabbing Hecate's hand, I pulled her with me to melt into the dark. Relief surged through me to see that we had indeed dissolved into the shadows. Now, I just had to picture the place we needed to go. I visualized the dining hall at the academy. I'd moved through the gloomy recesses and corners there a number of times. The first time I traveled from the underworld to the school, had been into that dining hall, so I knew it was possible to reach it.

With the image of the lofty ceiling and dark wooden tables firmly planted in my mind, I stepped through the shadows toward it, taking Hecate with me. As we moved, I instantly realized it hadn't worked. We ended up just on the other side of the cave instead.

"Shit!"

Hecate didn't look too surprised.

"Let's try again," I urged, pulling her into the darkness again.

This time, I pictured the hedge maze on the grounds of the academy. Maybe being outside would work better. It was a place I'd traveled to and from before, so there shouldn't have been any kind of road blockage. Closing my eyes, I saw the white wood and stone gazebo in my mind, as if I was right there. It was my favorite place at the school. Maybe the emotional connection would help.

I stepped toward it, reaching for it, longing for it. Yet, the moment I was out of the shadows, my fingertips touched bumpy rock, and I grasped that we were still in the cave. The disappointment of it weighed on my entire body.

"I told you, I tried everything." Hecate went to

crouch near the fire pit. She took the spit, pulling off the rest of the cooked carcass and put it into her mouth.

The sight of it made me shudder. I refused to accept that was my new reality.

"There has to be a way out."

She shrugged. "If there is, I don't know what it is."

"Have you run into others here? Surely, we can't be the only ones Nyx has trapped. She seems like a woman with a very volatile temper."

"You're the first one," she replied simply, absently chewing on the bone of whatever she'd cooked over the fire.

For some reason, I just couldn't believe that. Did I think she was lying? I wasn't sure. I didn't want to consider the ramifications of the possibility. Because if she had met others, where were they? What had happened to them?

Hecate got to her feet again and moved toward me. "The meadows are big, there could be others here somewhere, but it's so hard to see, so hard to walk around to find them."

"You found me easily enough," I challenged, suddenly conscious of the way she was eyeing me. She also had a very feline way about her, her movements graceful, yet predatory. I once saw a panther pounce on a gazelle in a documentary. Hecate reminded me of that panther.

"That's true." She smiled and the blood rushed out of my head.

I took a step back when she advanced, feeling

"She knows!" the gravely voice from under her hair shouted. "Don't let her get away!"

Before the full weight of that statement settled in my mind, I turned to run out of the cave. Hecate convulsed and shuddered, her whole body vibrating just as her head twisted—the other way this time.

Then she was leaping across the cave like a big cat, and the maw of her deformed, inhumane face gaped wide, razor sharp teeth dripping with saliva. That wide, lethal mouth came down, fangs sinking into the flesh of my shoulder.

I screamed.

CHAPTER THREE

MELANY

*P*ain seared me, sizzling down my arm like acid. The scent of blood, my blood, invaded my nose as I struggled to push Hecate off me. She was strong, and her grip on my shoulder was fierce. Her jaw closed like a vice on my shoulder. Any more pressure and I was certain she was going to sever my arm right off my body, or crack my clavicle bone in half.

Trying hard to overpower her, I punched at her stomach, sides and head. I backed her up into the wall, slamming her against it over and over, hoping something would give. It was pointless. Her teeth were firmly locked into my flesh, and her hands like claws clamped around my arms. She was like a mad dog with a taste for blood. I didn't think I could pry her off that way.

I summoned my powers, reaching for the first one that chose to surface. Fire erupted from my hands and I grabbed her by the hair, trying to yank her away. The flames scorched her long, dark strands, burning them to her scalp, but still, she kept biting me. I set my other hand around her neck, hoping to choke her out. The stench of her skin bubbling and blackening assaulted my senses.

Hecate's body started to convulse again, and she finally, thankfully, unhinged her mouth, a stomach-turning popping noise filled the cave as her fangs came out of my flesh. The relief was instant, despite the pain that still rippled through me.

She stumbled backward, hitting the back of her head against the rock wall, clutching and batting at her throat and head to put out the fire. Clenching my fists, I snuffed out the flames on her body, then tried to soothe her with a burst of my water power. The sizzle of water meeting fire echoed through the cave. Even though she tried to take a chunk out of my shoulder, I didn't want to kill her.

Thankfully she didn't hit an artery along my

collar bone with her teeth. If she had, I would've bled out in seconds. As it was, blood oozed out of the large puncture marks in my skin, rolled down my arm and dripped onto the cave floor. My whole arm ached, and the edges of the holes burned. Gods, what if it got infected? I didn't have Chiron around to make me drink some Gods-awful potion, or rub some stinking ointment on my wound—all the while lecturing me about not getting into dangerous situations.

I tore the other sleeve on my shirt, ripping it at the seams, and wrapped it around the bloody gore on my shoulder. It hurt, but I had to get it to stop bleeding. When I tied it off, I looked over at Hecate, who had failed to move from where she collapsed against the rock wall.

She was a motionless, dark lump in the shadows.

"I can't believe you just tried to eat me!"

Her body convulsed again, and I could see her head twisting to the side unnaturally, until her pale pretty face looked at me, her big eyes watery. Tears streamed down her cheeks. I tried not to look at the singed bristles of dark hair on her pale scalp, or the black burn on her neck.

"I-I'm so sorry. I don't know what came over

me." Her voice was raspy, and I wondered if it was from the damage I'd inflicted on her.

It was crazy to me that I could feel sorry for some great Goddess after she just tried to kill me. But I did. She looked so wilted and pathetic. Defeated. I supposed that was what being here for over three months could do to a person. I refused to end up like her. I would fight to my very last breath to escape this place.

She crawled over to me on her knees, scuttling like a crab. I cringed as she got closer. "I can heal you." She reached for my shoulder but I pulled away.

"Why should I trust you? Maybe you'll rip off my arm this time and cook it over the fire."

When she covered her face with both hands, and really started to cry, I began to wonder what kind of leftovers she'd eaten when we first came into the cave. I hated that I thought that, but she honestly gave me no choice. She'd tried to eat my shoulder. I shuddered remembering the sucking sounds she made as she supped on my blood.

The truth was, I should've been prepared for it. Lucian had told me what she'd done to take his blood when he required safe passage to the under-world, in search for me.

I felt bad standing there, watching her sob. Even though she'd been the one to attack me, guilt stabbed me in the gut. Either she was really upset, overcome with remorse at what she had done, or I was being a sucker by buying into it. I supposed it didn't matter, one way or another I needed some healing magic. That was one power I didn't possess. If Georgina was here, I knew she would fix me up *pronto*, but I didn't have her skills.

"I'm sorry about your hair and your neck," I finally offered, as a way to breach the awkwardness that her attack had created.

Sniffling, she looked up at me, a hand going to the singed strands on her head. "I deserved it."

"Can you not control...?" I pointed to the side of her head, where her "other" resided.

"Sometimes. But when I'm under a lot of stress, I guess she just takes over."

I nodded, wanting to believe her, but still wary. "If you can heal me, I'd appreciate it."

Scuttling over to the small fire pit, Hecate clapped her hands together, then blew on them toward the burnt wood. Small flames sparked in the center of the fire pit. After she blew on the flames some more, the old wood firmly caught fire.

As she rubbed her hands together again, a soft

green glow started to emerge. Chanting words I didn't understand under her breath, she spat something into her palms. After a few seconds, I realized it was blood. My stomach roiled, when it dawned on me that it was my blood that she'd just sucked out of my body.

Once she smeared it all over her hands, she set them over the fire. Every few seconds, she would lower them closer to the flames, until they were directly against the red glowing embers of the wood. Yet, her skin didn't burn and blacken like my fire had done to her.

Standing, although still slouched over as if in deference to me, Hecate came to my side. She gestured to my makeshift bandage, so I untied it and removed the cloth from my wounds, careful not to tear off the clots that had started to form.

When she set her hands over my wound, I sucked in a deep breath. The pain was instant, rippling over my skin, down my arm and spine, and settling right in my core. It started to fade a bit, replaced by a comforting warmth that spread across my entire body and I almost felt euphoric.

I couldn't stop the long drawn out sigh of relief. "Aww, that feels amazing."

She kept pressing her hands down. "I can teach

you to do this. You already have a fire power, it wouldn't take much for you to master the rest."

"I'm not sure I'd be comfortable performing blood magic," I admitted.

She nodded in understanding.

"Can you heal yourself?" I asked.

"Yes."

Another rush of relief surged over me. Now, I could stop feeling so guilty about burning off her hair and flesh.

When she was finished and released the hold on my shoulder, I rotated it, noticing how good it felt. There were still puncture marks in a semicircular row, but they were closing up, as if weeks had gone by and not just a few minutes. I didn't feel pain anymore, just a dull ache, like a toothache but in my clavicle.

"Thank you."

She shrugged. "It's the least I can do." Taking a few steps back to the fire, she settled her palms over the embers again. That time, Hecate set her hands on her head and throat. Like literal magic, the skin on her throat turned back to pink, a bit more tender looking but not the scorched flesh I'd given her, and her head looked better too. Her hair didn't suddenly become long again, but it was no longer in patches with bald spots in between.

When she was done, she gestured to the fire. "Keep the flames up, I'm going to go get us something to eat. You need to rest."

I was about to argue, wanting to get the hell out of there, but she was right, I needed some downtime to regain my strength. So, I just nodded, and she left the cave. When she was gone, I tended to the fire, drank some more water from the pool, and ate some berries.

Hecate returned not long after with a dead rodent that I couldn't identify. It looked somewhat like a rabbit, but had a bigger head and a bigger set of teeth. She gutted it with a makeshift knife she must've sharpened from a piece of shale rock, skinned it, then skewered it with the spit and set it over the fire.

As it cooked, she eyed me from under the fall of hair she still had on her head. "I understand why he took to you."

I frowned. "Who?"

"Hades."

At the mere mention of his name, my heart started to race. I opened my mouth to ask, but shut it again, unsure if I truly wanted to know the reason for her statement.

"You're strong. Stubborn. Tenacious." She turned the meat on the spit. "And I can see darkness in you. It was the same with Persephone."

There was an instant twinge of jealousy when Hecate mentioned the Goddess. Hades had lived for several millennia, I wasn't an idiot to think I was the first, but somewhere deep down inside I'd hoped I was special. That it was ME he'd fallen for deeply. That only I could make his heart feel something he'd never felt.

But that was naïve. Persephone had been there before me. I knew that. I'd seen the way he'd look at the painting of her in his bedroom, and the way his eyes would darken when he spoke about her.

"Did you know her well?"

She nodded. "Oh, yes. I was instrumental in negotiating the terms of her residence in the underworld with him."

"I'd heard stories that he'd taken her against her will to live with him."

She smirked. "No, that was not how it was with them. She fell for him as deeply as he fell for her. It was her mother, Demeter, who fought so hard against their relationship. She hated that Persephone loved Hades, and wanted to forsake the life she could've had on the earthly plain for one in darkness with him."

That didn't surprise me. Demeter had never hidden her disdain for Hades, and I knew it was rooted in Persephone's relationship with him. Yet, I never thought that Persephone had given everything up for him.

Was I going down the same path, even though he wasn't alive?

If someone asked Lucian and my friends, they'd probably say that was true.

"It was Zeus, wasn't it? The one who turned her against him?" I asked, although I knew the answer.

Hecate nodded. "Yes. Zeus had always been fiercely jealous of his brother. Hades bowed to no one, and that always bothered him."

A small smile blossomed across my face. That had been one of the many things I'd loved about Hades. Although sometimes it bothered me that he was so full of himself, so incredibly, frustratingly arrogant. Despite all of that, I still longed deeply for him. I was afraid I wasn't ever going to shake the feeling, that it would always take up space in my mind and in my heart. Maybe, I didn't have room in my heart for anyone else.

That made me think about Lucian, and I got sad. He really didn't deserve to be second best in anyone's eyes.

When the meat was done, Hecate tore off some chunks, then handed the rest to me. I'd never eaten roasted rodent before, but my stomach didn't care. I was hungry and I needed the energy it would provide me. A yawn escaped me once I finished. Fatigue was starting to settle on me.

"You should get some sleep," Hecate suggested.

"I want to find a way out."

"I know, but you must rest first."

Before I could argue further, Hecate blew across her hand toward me. Instantly, I felt sleep take hold. She was beside me before I could fall over onto my side, and gently laid me down onto the cave's floor.

"Sleep, and then you can leave."

CHAPTER FOUR

MELANY

*L*ucian was out on the training field with Heracles. They were practicing their hand to hand moves. The sunlight made his hair shimmer like polished gold and my fingers ached to brush through the silky strands.

I was suddenly struck by the way his beautiful body moved. The muscles in his arms and chest rippled when he went to strike Heracles, laughing when the big God sidestepped him and tried to push him off balance. His movements were so quick, full of grace and confidence. Either I'd forgotten how majestic he was, or I'd never truly recognized it before.

Lucian was perfection. A golden God himself. I didn't deserve him. I never had.

I watched him and Heracles spar for a little longer, surprised Lucian hadn't noticed my arrival. Usually, he knew the instant I was around, and would come to wrap me in his strong arms.

Lifting my hand, I waved. "Lucian!"

His head didn't turn my way. Maybe he hadn't heard me.

"Hey, Lucian! Are you ignoring me or something?"

Still, he didn't react, or even make any notice that he'd heard me.

Frowning, I turned to see Jasmine and Georgina come out of the side door of the academy, and run onto the field. Shocked, I noticed Georgina outfitted with the mechanical arm I'd commissioned Hephaistos to make. Had he finished it and already given it to her when I disappeared? Surely, I hadn't been gone that long. Besides, he wouldn't do that to me; he knew I'd want to give it to her myself. Despite his gruffness, I considered the forge God to be a friend.

Jasmine's hair was short, a mass of tight curls on her head. When had she gotten it cut? She'd always told me she'd never cut her hair short, that she liked her long dark waves.

Laughing together, they made a beeline toward Lucian, not even looking my way.

"Yo, Gina! Jasmine!" I waved, while trying to move my leg so I could walk toward them, but my leg wouldn't lift. I was stuck on that spot, as if my feet were frozen to the ground beneath me. What was going on?

With their arrival, Lucian and Heracles ended their training, and Lucian joined Jasmine and Georgina. "What's up?" he asked.

"I thought since we're all going to the same place for training today, we could go together," Georgina offered.

"Right." Lucian nodded. "I almost forgot we started the elemental instruction today."

"How could you forget that? It's kind of a big deal." Jasmine held out her hand and a ball of fire formed in the center.

I frowned. How did Jasmine get her fire powers back? I was definitely happy to see it, but I was confused on how it happened. Chiron and I had been struggling for months, trying to find a way to return what my friends had given me in the battle.

"Sometimes I question the wisdom in letting us teach the next gen of recruits." Jasmine laughed as she tossed the ball of fire into the air, caught it, and snuffed it out by simply closing her hand.

"Cuz we won the battle, vanquished the typhon, and saved the academy. It's just good PR, having the Heroes of Pecunia teach the next set of heroes." Lucian struck a pose like he was modeling for a photo op, then he started to laugh.

A few more people streamed out when the side door to the academy opened again. I instantly recognized the girl with the wild red hair— Cassandra—but when I noticed who walked beside her, my knees buckled, and I dropped to the ground.

Her dark, wavy hair swung along her chin as she gestured with her hands, then smiled as Cassandra said something to her. I'd hardly ever seen Revana smile, so it was doubly disturbing to see her now, in front of me, walking, talking animatedly, and... *alive*.

Once they got closer, I could actually hear her voice. "I'll see you later. I've got to help Hermes with flying class today."

"Good luck," Cassandra responded as Revana's large red wings expanded out from her back and she took to the air.

The others walked toward Cassandra. Lucian waved to Revana, and she waved back with a smile. My gut churned again at the sight.

"Where's she going?" Lucian asked Cassandra.

"Flying class, I guess."

Nodding, Lucian reached out, hooked an arm around Cassandra's waist, and pulled her close to him. Giggling, she draped her arms around his neck and they kissed. It was a long, deep kiss reserved for couples who were familiar with each other.

Couples who were in love…

All thought and reason seeped out of my head in a heady rush, and I was left feeling faint and sick to my stomach. "What the hell is going on?!" I shouted from where I crouched on the ground, my legs still ineffectual to hold me up.

Flinching, Cassandra turned her head in my direction, and frowned. "Did anyone hear that?"

"Hear what?" Lucian asked.

"I thought I heard a girl shouting or something."

Did she hear me? I got to my feet, and waved

my hands in the air. "Cassandra! It's Melany. Can you hear me?!"

Her frown deepened, and she pulled out of Lucian's arms, a hand going up to her head.

"Are you okay?" Lucian asked, holding her lower back. "Are you having another vision?"

Cassandra shook her head. "No, it doesn't feel like that. It feels different."

"Cassandra!!! HELP ME get out of here!!" I shouted with every ounce of energy I had.

Wincing, she grabbed her head in both hands. "Stop it! Get out of my head!"

Suddenly, a wave of power surged over me, shoving me backward. My eyes blinked open, and I found myself staring into a wall of gray mist just outside the cave that I'd been in with Hecate. Confused, I turned to glance around me.

Why was I here? Hadn't I just been asleep in the cave?

A creeping sensation rippled over me and I whipped around to see Hecate standing nearby, watching me. "Was I sleepwalking? I had the strangest dream about my friends back at the academy. It seemed like they didn't know me."

"It wasn't a dream, Melany."

"Sure it was. I was asleep and…"

She shook her head. "You saw the present. You saw what is happening right now at the academy."

My stomach started to churn at the implications. "I don't understand."

"You don't exist to them. It's as if you were never there."

"But I was there. I stayed in a room with Gina. Jasmine and I went to Pecunia together, Lucian and I…" I licked my lips, feeling the weight of what she was saying crush my heart. "We were together. We fought together in the battle of Pecunia. They all gave me their powers so I could defeat Zeus."

"Being in Asphodel Meadows means you don't exist in the real world, and never did. They have no memory of you. All of that time together, all of those specials moments, all those conversations and intimate rendezvous, never happened to them."

I shook my head vehemently, I couldn't accept what she was saying to me. It was impossible. "No. I don't believe you. It happened. I remember it."

"Maybe in another reality it happened, but not in their reality."

Standing, I paced around in front of her, trying to wrap my mind around her words. "That's not right. You said you've been here for months. Well, I remembered you. Lucian told me about you and what he had to do to find me in the underworld. They remember you. I remember you coming to Hades's Hall and fighting with us against Zeus and the typhon. So if you were here and had been erased, how can we remember you?"

"Because I'm a Goddess, and I can't be erased. I've been here when time and memory and death were born. For mortals and demigods and creatures it is this way, but for Gods we can be imprisoned here forever, but we will always exist.

The pain in my gut worsened. I could feel it churning like a washing machine. Bile rose in my throat, and I dropped to my knees and retched. I threw up every meager thing I'd eaten in the past few hours, which wasn't much, but was enough to fill my mouth with an awful rancid taste.

Wiping my mouth with the back of my hand, I got to my feet and blindly ran into the fog.

"Melany! Where are you going?" Hecate called after me, but her voice soon faded into the mist as I pumped my legs as hard and fast as they could go, vanishing into the floating grayness of the meadows.

I didn't know where I was running to, I had no

plan, all I knew was I had to get away from Hecate and her words. Away from the images that still lingered in my mind—of my friends, of Lucian and Cassandra. The sight of their lips touching circled around and around, making my head spin.

Eventually, I came upon the river again. I wasn't sure how long or how far I ran, but I dropped to my knees on the shore and stared at the rushing water —its sound buzzing in my ears. It would be so easy to cup the water in my hands and drink. To have my memories fade into oblivion. This pain in my heart, and nausea in my belly could go away. Like magic, it would be like it never existed. Like Lucian, Jasmine, Georgina and the others never existed...

The memory of Hades could be erased. I'd never feel that gnawing ache in my mind, body, and soul ever again. Like Nyx, snapping her fingers to send me here, those feelings would vanish into a gray abyss. I would stop being haunted by my memories of him.

My hands dipped into the cold water, and I looked at it, rippling in my hold. I could just lift them to my lips, tilting them up ever so slightly to let the cool liquid fill my mouth and roll down my throat.

Except, then I'd languish here in this place with

no desire to leave. With no reason to get back to reality.

No. I wouldn't do it.

Pulling my hands out of the river, I wiped them dry on my pants.

"I'm sorry to have to tell you the truth."

I stood, and turned to face Hecate, who'd crept up silently behind me. She had that way of moving, like her feet never had to touch the ground.

"If we return to that reality, will we exist again? Will my friends remember me? Will the past realign itself?"

Her shoulders lifted and fell with uncertainty. "I honestly don't know. It's impossible to say. How can we ever know if someone was here and came back, if we never even knew they were gone?"

"Well, I aim to put that to the test. I refuse to stay here in this place. Tomorrow, I'm going to find a way out... even if it kills me."

Hecate nodded. "I understand. I will help you find a way."

I narrowed my eyes at her, seeing her shrink into herself. The guilt of what she'd done to me, and maybe to others, weighed on her so much that it seemed to literally be crushing her. "You're coming with me, Hecate. I won't let you stay here."

She gave me a soft smile and nodded, but there was a look in her eyes that told me that, quite possibly, she hadn't told me the entire truth. She was hiding something else from me.

CHAPTER FIVE

LUCIAN

I was back in the battle with the chimera that nearly razed the entire Victory Forest to cinders. I was in the air, zipping around its three heads, trying to electrocute it but having no luck. The beast seemed impervious to my lightning.

Turning its lion head, it breathed a line of fire at the treeline, setting everything ablaze. Jasmine's wing caught fire when she flew in its path, and she was forced to drop to the ground, patting at the feathers to snuff it.

Others, like Su and Quinn, attempted to get the firefights out of harm's way. As Quinn picked up one of the men to airlift him out of the forest, the air nearby seemed to open like a wound in someone's flesh, and Cerberus—the large, black, three-headed dog that belonged to Hades and the underworld—bounded out of it. On his back, he carried the three Furies, winged bat-like women, and a young woman with wild blue hair, dressed all in black.

The sight of her took my breath in an instant, and I was filled with such fierce emotion that I didn't know how to react. Even in my dream, I sucked in air in an attempt to control the racing of my heart. I didn't know her, but I felt so enamored with that woman that it hurt.

The three Furies took to the air in an instant. With triple shrieks that vibrated in my ears, they shot toward the chimera, weapons brandished, ready for battle. Cerberus charged toward the hovering beast, but it ducked out of his way just as three sets of jaws snapped in the air. He let out a loud, earth-shaking bark, all three heads moving in unison.

Stunned, I watched as this warrior girl flew into the air, her huge black wings flapping as she nocked an arrow in her bow. "Get the others out of the forest!" she shouted at the hell hound.

It was then, as she turned her head, that I could see a network of scars on her cheek and along one side of her neck. She also had tattoos on her arms. I'd never seen someone so fierce looking before, and so attractive all at once.

The dog obeyed. Did Hades send these people to help with the battle? Did this woman command the creatures of the underworld just as the God of Darkness did? If he had sent them to help, it would've been a first. All the rumors about Hades hadn't painted him to be a generous soul. He was Zeus's and Poseidon's brother, but as far as I knew he didn't have anything to do with the academy.

She let the arrow fly. The chimera maneuvered out of its way, but it ended up in the path of one of the Furies. The blood-haired demigod sliced the creature across the back leg, and it let out a pained roar. Swiftly, the blue-haired girl flew toward me with a smile, tossing me a spear. Without wasting a moment, I caught it, and dove toward the chimera that the Furies now had circled.

With a fierce thrust, I stabbed it in the flank, just as another arrow came whizzing by, sinking into the left eye on the goat's head. The Furies let out a collective war cry that startled me a bit, then flew at the chimera—swords and spears advancing.

The beast turned its lion head just at the Fury with the black hair dove at it. Its large mouth opened, and it blasted a stream of fire. Unfortunately, the Fury didn't have a chance to duck. The fire immediately caught her wings, burning them to ash, and she dropped like a dead weight. The redheaded sister caught her before she could hit the ground, then she shot back into the air with her sword aimed at the chimera's side.

"Cut its wings," the blue-haired girl shouted.

The Fury swooped under the beast and veered upward, her sword tearing through its right appendage. The creature banked to the left, toward me. I rolled down toward the ground, almost colliding with it, but was able to get out of the way. Still, the action sent me very close to the rocky side of the cavern. I managed to pull out of my tuck and I soared upward, my wings spread wide.

I was fully aware that the warrior woman was staring at me, an intensity in her eyes, and it made my gut clench—and other parts of my body take notice. Logically, I didn't know her, but my dream body sure did, and reacted to her on such a primal level that it was impossible for it not to take over.

Our connection broke when the Fury with the green hair flew at the chimera, an injured Jasmine with her, and swiped high then low with her sword. The blade caught the left pinion, tearing a hole in the leathery webbing. The beast listed to the side again, struggling to stay in the air.

It was definitely an opportunity to take the chimera down, and the blue haired girl saw that. Slinging her bow over her shoulder, she unsheathed a long broad sword. She was the most breathtaking, magnificent, and terrifying person I'd ever seen as she swooped toward the chimera. Dodging the stream of fire that spewed from its mouth, she feigned right as the beast went left, but whipped around at the last second, bringing down her sword with a fierce blow. The blade sliced right through the lion's neck.

The chimera instantly fell to the ground, its lion's head rolling across the blackened landscape. Blood stained the soil, seeping into it like dark red ink. Once it was down, the Furies sprung on it to finish the job.

I watched as the blue-haired warrior descended to the ground, her gaze searching for me. Our eyes locked on each other and another wave of intense emotion surged through me.

Who was that woman? Why did she have such a hold on me?

I didn't know, but in the dream, I was enraptured by her.

Slowly, I landed too, smiling at the girl, feeling triumphant at the chimera's demise. Something hit me then. It was like being struck with a metal, spiked baseball bat across the shoulder blades. The pain was sudden and instant. A burning, but not from fire. No. Whatever that was infected my blood, and like acid, it seared my insides from my head to my feet.

As my body convulsed, I cried out, flinging a hand out toward the girl, reaching for her to save me. Thinking that, somehow, she could.

"Nooo!" Screaming, she sprinted toward me. Her sword already in motion, she lopped of the snake tail that had bitten me. I dropped to the ground, but she caught me in her arms before I could hit the rocky edge of the gorge and fall into it.

Gently, the girl settled me on the ground, my body quivering across her lap. I couldn't stop shaking as the venom coursed through me, shutting down my organs one by one. I'd be dead soon, that I already knew.

Although I didn't want to die, I really didn't want to leave her. "Blue…" I gasped, unsure exactly why I said that. Was that her name?

"Don't talk," she whispered, rocking me in her arms. "Save your energy. It's going to be okay." Tears rolled down her pale blood-streaked cheeks. I so wanted to lift a hand and wipe them away.

The Furies, and Jasmine gathered around us.

"Help him," she begged Jasmine.

Unfortunately, she could only press her lips together as she cried. "I don't know what to do."

The flapping sound of wings reached us when others landed nearby. Ren ran to our side, kneeling down to touch my face. "What happened?"

The warrior girl opened her mouth, but no words escaped. She looked like she was in shock, and I wanted to console her even as I felt the life slipping away from me.

"The chimera's snake bit him in the back," Jasmine answered through sobs.

As gently as he could, Ren rolled me a bit so he could look at my back, but I could see his throat swallowing the hard truth.

The girl started to cry even harder and she ran a hand over my face. "It's okay, baby. You're going to be okay."

"Blue..." My hand lifted, weakly cupping her cheek. "I love you."

"Someone help me!" she screamed.

With her voice I felt a darkness coming. It floated over me and swallowed me whole. Except, she—the fierce warrior woman—was there with me.

She remained with me, in the shadows...

I jolted straight up on the bed, my throat dry, my breathing ragged. Unsteady, my hands ran over my sweaty face, and I swung my legs over the side of the cot. My heart raced, and I swore I could still feel the sting of the chimera's bite along my shoulder blades. Reaching over my shoulder, I touched my bare back to make sure there was nothing there. My skin was as smooth as it always had been. The only marks there, were the thin slats along my shoulder blades where my wings emerged.

I'd never had a dream that vivid before. I wondered if Dionysus spiked the punch at the impromptu jam session he put on last night, in the dining hall. My head was pounding like I had drank too much.

Getting up, I did some push-ups and crunches to blow the cobwebs off, then dressed in my usual training gear and went down to the dining hall for breakfast. Everyone was already there when I arrived. After getting a tray and scooping up some eggs, toast, and oatmeal, I sat at our usual table.

Cassandra frowned at me when I took the chair beside her. "Everything okay? Your aura is all fuzzy."

"I, ah, had the most vivid dream."

She didn't say anything, but she did get kind of quiet. "About what?"

"It was really weird. It was about that time we battled the chimera last year…"

Jasmine, Georgina, Ren and Diego all perked up as I told the story.

"That was crazy," Jasmine agreed. "Sometimes my wing still aches a bit."

"Anyway, it was the battle, but there was this girl there. A girl with blue-hair and black wings. She just kind of showed up with Cerberus and the Furies, and basically slaughtered the chimera."

"She stole your glory, bro," Ren joked.

"Were the Furies as gruesome in your dream as we've heard about?" Jasmine asked.

I shrugged, feeling stupid after telling them about my dream. It all sounded so ridiculous. "I don't know. They kinda looked like bats but one had red hair, one had black, and one had green."

"Stylish bats, who knew?" Jasmine laughed, the others joined her.

"This girl with the blue hair, was she hot?"

Diego waggled his eyebrows at me, then his gaze went to Cassandra who had yet to respond. He stopped messing around.

"It was just really intense, that's all."

Once I finished my breakfast, we all got to our respective duties in the academy. Cassandra seemed a bit distracted when I hugged her goodbye. I had elemental training with the new recruits. Since Zeus's untimely departure, it was up to me now to teach everyone how to create and control lightning.

Ren got in the pool with Poseidon while I stood on the top ramp in the elemental building, next to the lightning rods that protruded through the ceiling. Georgina helped Demeter with manipulating plants and rocks, and Jasmine aided Hephaistos in teaching the new recruits about handling fire.

The only God teaching on his own was Erebus, who worked with the recruits on how to create and use the shadows. There wasn't another recruit at the academy that possessed the ability to manipulate the shadows like Erebus could. It was a power for those born to the darkness.

Thinking about shadows, made me think about the blue-haired girl from my dream again. I wasn't sure why. Although, it could've been the way she was dressed, and how she seemed to command or at

least ally with those who existed in the darkness—
like Cerberus and the Furies.

I was so distracted by my thoughts of her, I
nearly electrocuted one of my students.

After class, I flew to the hedge maze outside of
academy to meet up with Cassandra. It was sort of
our spot. It was where we first met, when
Prometheus brought the new recruits on a tour of
the grounds. I'd just happened to be sitting in the
gazebo, doing some meditation when they came
through the path.

I'd noticed her, with her wild red hair and
intense gaze, immediately. I had been drawn to her.

Cassandra was already there, sitting in the
gazebo when I landed next to it. I walked up the
few steps into the pale stone and wood structure,
smiling, but she didn't return my smile. Something
was up, so I sat next to her when she didn't get up
to greet me.

"What's going on?"

"You know that blue-haired girl you dreamt
about?" She looked down at the floor as she spoke.

I nodded.

"I dreamt about her too last night."

"What? How is that possible? Are you sure it
was the same girl?"

"Short, choppy blue hair, blue eyes, black wings, tattoos, and a spiderweb type scarring along one side of her face and down her neck? Kind of looked like a lightning pattern?"

Swallowing, I nodded.

"In my dream, the blue haired girl was sparring with Medusa in the eastern training field. They were fighting like they were both enemies and allies, if that makes any sense. You were there, as was Jasmine, Gina, and the others. You were cheering her on. And the way... the way you looked at her, I could tell that you were in love with her." She turned her head slightly to glance at me, probably to gauge my reaction to that.

My hands scrubbed my face. I didn't know what was happening. It was too weird. "What does it mean?"

Cassandra shook her head. "I don't know."

"Is it one of your visions?"

She licked her lips, her face contorting as if her next words would change everything. "I'm not sure, it almost feels like a memory."

Meeting her gaze, I reluctantly nodded. I had thought the same thing.

Ever since I woke from the dream, notions about the blue-haired girl stayed with me. Like I thought that she was originally from Pecunia, and her favorite food was pancakes with a lot of chocolate sauce and whipped cream piled on top. Why I thought that, I didn't know, but it stuck.

I also thought about how her skin felt under my fingers, and the smell of her hair. It was so powerful that it disturbed me. How could I have these memories of someone I didn't know?

CHAPTER SIX

MELANY

*a*fter resting a bit in the cave, eating the rest of the rodent Hecate cooked, and filling a makeshift canteen with the safe water from the pool, we set out to find a way out of the meadows. I was determined despite the odds stacked against us.

Hecate had said that she walked along the river and couldn't find a way out of there. It wasn't that I didn't believe her, but I needed to see it for myself. Lucian had always held that I was one of the most stubborn people he ever knew.

Lucian.

I sighed. I hoped I could get back, and he would

remember me again. Seeing him with all our friends, and with Cassandra, had been a punch to the gut. It was hard knowing everything that had happened to him, them, and the academy had occurred without me.

Their future had changed without me as well. For the better? I couldn't say. Or basically, I didn't really want to consider that notion.

We left the cave and trudged toward the river. It was slow going as the fog seemed to get thicker. A defense mechanism? Quite possibly. I could barely see my hand before my face, let alone the ground at my feet. We walked very close together, so we didn't lose sight of each other.

When we reached the river's edge, we started going north along its bank. Everything looked the same—same small rocks, scrub, wildflowers with no real color—nothing to distinguish how far we'd gotten. We could've been moving within one spot, in an endless gray loop for all I knew.

Also, I couldn't tell how long we'd been gone. I needed something to help me tell the passage of time. It would most definitely ground me, and stop me from going mad. Since there was no sun or moon to cross the sky, I needed something else, like an hourglass.

Hecate nearly bumped into me when I stopped and looked at the ground. Kicking the pebbles, I realized there was some sandy dirt along the shore. Crouching, I tore at my other sleeve, made a little pouch that I could tie to my belt. I filled it with the sand.

"What are you doing?" Hecate asked.

"Making a clock. I can't handle not knowing if time has passed or not."

Once it was secure to my belt, I poked a tiny hole in the bottom so the sand could slowly drain out. When the pouch was empty, I'd know that a certain amount of time had passed. I would think of it as a sand hour. Then, we started walking again.

After three sand hours had passed, I started to feel weird—Disassociated from my body in a way. Like floating. My legs were on autopilot, putting one foot in front of the other, my arms swinging ever so slightly, my head bobbing to the monotonous motion. My mind drifted, and I started to think about Hades.

I knew I should have been thinking about Lucian and my friends, but when untethered, my thoughts automatically went toward the God of the

Underworld, how much I missed him, and how I longed to be with him still.

The thought of the first time I saw him bloomed in my mind, when he just appeared in the auditorium at the academy, claiming me as his apprentice. I'd been shocked, but secretly thrilled at the possibilities. He had intrigued me during those few unexpected meetings at the gazebo in the maze, as he strummed his guitar, and looked at me with that way he had. When he took me without warning through the shadows, I'd fought, kicked, and screamed at the gull of his ego, but deep down, I had been inflamed with a passion I had no idea had existed.

Something inside me had ignited and it hadn't ever stopped burning.

So wrapped up in my memories, I didn't see the large boulders stacked up on the river's edge, and I ran smack into them. My knees buckled and I tumbled to the ground, nearly rolling into the water. Hecate managed to grab me by the arm before I did, yanking me back.

Startled, I blinked up at her. "Thanks."

"You need to watch where you are walking," she chided, helping

"It's hard in this place. Everything looks the same."

"That is how it wears you down. How it lulls you into accepting your fate, and drinking the water."

I looked down at the rushing river, acutely aware that I almost succumbed to it. "When you drink, do you just lose your memories? Does something else happen?"

Swallowing, Hecate nodded. "It's said that if you drink the Waters of Forgetfulness, you not only forget who you are, but what you are."

My brows wrinkled in concern. That sounded menacing, but I was afraid to ask exactly what it meant. I thanked her again for saving me, and we got back onto the trail to keep advancing along the river.

Once two more sand hours passed, I decided to stop for a drink of water from the canteen. My stomach also rumbled, and I wondered if Hecate knew where we could get more berries. I was about to ask her, when I spied a dark form undulating in the gray mist—about six feet to the left of where we stood.

I wondered whether Hecate saw the same form, when she grabbed my arm and nodded toward another shadowy shape moving down stream from us. I looked up stream, and found more activity. Were they animals or people? Maybe something else altogether. With the way Hecate tensed against me, her fingernails digging into my flesh in warning, I was betting on the latter.

I immediately called my powers to the surface. Sparks buzzed around my fingers, just as the skin on my hands heated—my fire ability simmered just below. My powers were a bit muted, but I hoped they would be enough to combat whatever was coming out of the fog.

We didn't have long to wait as three, no, four black shapes floated toward us. They seemed humanoid, but that was where the familiarity ended. They actually appeared to be shadows, with wisps of arms and legs as mere suggestions of what limbs should look like.

"Shades," Hecate whispered.

"What are they?"

"They used to be people. Mortals, demigods, Gods, I'm not sure which." She stepped closer to me as the one on her left got near. "Anyone who drank the water from the river. This what happens to them. They become apparitions. They forget that they were ever people."

"What do they want?"

"To feed on our energy. To take over our bodies."

Awesome. Just awesome. "How do we kill them?"

"We have to fill them with what they fear most."

I turned to gawk at her. "What the hell is that supposed to mean?"

Before she could answer, one of the shades lunged at her, but Hecate was quick to counter the attack with a blast of magic. The beam of green energy surged from her hands, going right through the spectre, and slowing it down enough for her to get out of its way.

I wasn't as lucky. The shade closest to me was able to enshroud me before I could blast it with a bolt of lightning. It surrounded me like a shadow but it was so cold, icy, bitter, and I immediately started to shiver.

Calling on the fire that waited just beneath my skin, bright flames ignited in my hands. Instantly, I formed a fire ball between them and blindly flung it out, not knowing if I was hitting anything significant.

"Melany!" Hecate's voice was faint and muffled, as if coming from outside a room. "Be careful!

They can fool you into believing—" Her words cut off before she could finish the sentence.

I whirled around left then right, trying to figure out how I could get away from this shade, but there didn't seem to be a corporeal version of it that I could escape. It was smoke and darkness all around me, nothing I could grab hold of and yank. It acted very much like the shadows I was used to, the darkness I'd become accustomed to, and that made me think about Hades again.

"Hello, Melany."

His voice came from behind me, and I spun to see him materialize from the dark mist. He was there, standing in front of me, his dark hair slicked back from his beautiful, angular face. He wore one of his usually expensive dark suits, and a crisp, white, buttoned-up shirt with a collar.

"Hades?"

He smiled. It was slow and lazy, and it made my belly clench so hard I nearly gasped.

Closing the gap between us, I lifted a hand to touch his face. He was real. I sighed in relief when I felt the stubble along his chin under my fingers. "How are you here?"

"Not sure, actually." He shrugged his shoulders,

then ran a hand over his suit jacket. "I thought I was gone for good."

My arms wrapped around him, and I buried my face into his chest with such force that I nearly knocked him backward. I could feel tears welling in my eyes. I couldn't believe he was here, and that I had my arms around him.

A hand stroked the back of my head. "I take it you missed me."

"Yes, I missed you, you ass." I raised my head to look him in the eyes. "Where did you go? I saw you turn to ash right in front of me. I looked for you, thinking you were in Elysium."

He shrugged. "I don't know. But I'm here now, and that's what's important." His hand came around to cup my cheek, angling my chin up to his. "Kiss me. Show me how much you missed me."

I didn't hesitate, and my lips were on his.

The kiss was everything I'd hoped it would be. Hot, wet, and deep. I moaned into him, my whole body melting in his arms.

His other hand came up to my face, cupping the other cheek, and he deepened the kiss. After a few seconds, everything started to feel strange. It felt like he was holding me so I wouldn't move, so he could sweep his tongue over mine.

Suddenly, I started to choke. Like the air was being sucked from my lungs.

Both hands against his chest, I tried to push him back, but he was strong and held me firmly. What was going on? What was he doing to me? I attempted to speak against his mouth. I strained to say '*no, stop!*' but I couldn't get the words out of me. At that point, I was having trouble even breathing.

"Fight Melany…"

Hecate's voice pierced the veil of darkness around me. Her words coming in fits and starts.

"…use your gifts."

With her urgent words I called up the fire, trying to set his clothes ablaze, but the flames didn't seem to take. There was a small burst, and then it went out like someone had blown hard. Concentrating, I reached for the lightning zipping through me, but again, it fizzled and didn't produce the effect that I desired.

I was running out of options, as I felt my life force being drained away. This was what Hecate had warned me against. The shade had taken on the form of the one person I would gladly and happily cling to. It had used my most intimate desires and thoughts against me.

Fire and lightning were the abilities I always

used, because they were easy and simple to manipulate, but I had other weapons inside me. Powers my friends had given to me with trust. I reached for them next, hoping beyond hope that I found something that would save my life.

Focusing on the ground beneath me, I searched for an element to use. I found tree roots way down deep, but I didn't think they would be helpful. There was nothing for them to wrap around and crush. There were other components in the earth that I touched. Oxygen and silicon that made up the rocks. Other minerals came up, until I found what I was looking for—Iron.

Siphoning it from the dirt, I pulled harshly and drew it up, forging a type of wall. The moment the iron touched the shadows around me, I felt them shrink away.

Hades—or the apparition's aberration of him—lurched away from me. When his lips left mine, I dropped to the ground, taking in as many greedy gulps of air as I could. As I continued to struggle to breathe, I drew more iron from the earth. The more I constructed, the more the shade quivered around me. I could feel its pain while the element surrounded it, encasing it in a metal prison.

Eventually, the shadows about me dissipated

and solidified back into one form.

Coming to my side, Hecate helped me to my feet. "Now that you've imprisoned it, you have to kill it."

I swallowed. "How?" My throat hurt, but I was still able to choke out the question.

"Push it into the river. That is what it fears the most. That which took its soul."

I was shaky on my feet, but I knew I had to do what Hecate suggested, or else the shade would come back to literally haunt me. Its dark form quivered inside the iron cage I'd put it in, knowing what I was going to do.

Grabbing the iron bars I'd created, I dragged the cage to the river's edge. Before I sent it over, a face formed inside the black silhouette. Hade's face.

"Don't kill me, Melany. I love you. We can be together forever."

"You are already dead."

Blinking back tears, I shoved the shade into the river. Within seconds, the iron structure sunk into the river's depths, taking the shade with it. The water was like acid to the shadow monster; it bubbled as the cage sank. I could hear its desperate shrieks and the rattling of the bars on the cage as it fought to get out, but it was pointless.

CHAPTER SEVEN

MELANY

*a*fter we made sure the shade was gone, Hecate helped me over to the outcropping of rocks and I sat down, resting my back against one of the smooth stones. She handed me the canteen and I drank a few mouthfuls, not wanting to waste it.

"Are you all right?" she asked.

Without looking at her, I nodded, because I felt foolish having been tricked. "How did you get rid of the other shades?"

"I didn't. They all kind of converged on you as one."

"So, I destroyed them all in the river?"

"It looks like it." Taking a sip of water, she sat down beside me.

I scrubbed at my face and sighed, angry at myself. "I should've known it wasn't real. I can't believe how stupid I was."

"It knew what emotions to feed on. The ones that drive you."

My gaze got lost over the river, and around the gray mist that constantly just hung in the air, obscuring everything. "I wanted him to be alive so badly that I disregarded every ounce of reason I had. I knew it wasn't really him. I knew it." I slapped my hand down on my leg in frustration. "So stupid."

"Yes, it was stupid," a low, gravelly voice agreed, coming from under the dark fall of Hecate's stringy hair.

With a shake of her head, Hecate scowled. "Don't listen to her. She's always surly."

"She's right though. I need to let go. I need to stop hanging onto the hope that Hades is alive somewhere."

"I understand your suffering," Hecate admitted, "I too lost someone, and searched for them all over the different realms."

"Did he die?"

She shook her head. "No, *she* was transformed into an animal and cast out into the world."

"Who would do such a thing?" Although I asked, I already had an inkling of the answer. There were only so many people in the world who could be that cruel, and I'd battled one in particular the entire time I was at the academy.

Hecate gave me a knowing look. "Aphrodite transformed my lover, Gale, into a polecat when she refused to perform a curse on someone Aphrodite wanted to punish. So, she was punished instead."

"I'm so sorry, Hecate. That's awful."

"I've searched for her all over the world, in the underworld, even in the Temple of Night before Nyx snapped me to this place. I've even searched for her here. But I've been all over the meadows— from the hills to the lake—and I've never seen her." Sighing, she rested the back of her head against the rocks. "The only thing in that lake is the hydra, and it's not friendly at all."

I perked up at that, it was so unexpected. "You've seen the hydra?"

She nodded. "Yes, all nine of its heads."

A bit of a thrill rushed through me. "There's

only one hydra, right? Like, there aren't a whole bunch of them, like the cyclopses?"

"Yes, there is only one." Her eyes narrowed at me.

"Then, how can it be here, and in the lake near the academy?" No longer feeling tired, sore, or defeated, I got to my feet. Feeling invigorated by the possibility of what Hecate had just told me, I offered her my hand to pull her to her feet. "Show me this lake."

I followed Hecate down the river, over a few rolling hills, and then a vast valley where—after moving through the floating mist—I saw a large pool of water. A few trees dotted the shore.

It was the lake.

As I ran across the meadow to the lakeside, I couldn't stifle my excitement at the possibility at getting the hell out of here. This could be it. This could be the way home. If there was only one hydra, and it was here even though I'd seen it in the lake at the academy, that meant it had a way to cross from one lake to the other. If it could cross, then Hecate and I could cross too.

Gazing out over the still surface of the water, I willed the appearance of its nine heads. I'd never wanted to see a beast so badly in my life than I did right then. Well, that wasn't completely true. If I could see Cerberus right now, I'd be ecstatic.

"Do you remember when you saw it last?"

"I'm not sure. Time is a blur in my mind. But it was fairly early in my days here I believe."

I supposed it didn't matter when she saw it last. It wasn't like I could look at the calendar in my cell to make a timetable for the hydra's coming and goings. The only thing we could do was stand there, watch the water and wait.

"Do you see any of those berry bushes around?" I asked Hecate. "I'm hungry, and I suspect we're going to be sitting here a while."

"I did see a couple on the way here. I'll go pick some." Leaving me by the shore, she went to go find the bushes.

When she was gone, I sat cross-legged on the grassy terrain. I was still lightheaded and tired from almost having my life sucked out of me by the shades, but I was buoyed by the slight chance of finding a way out of here.

I picked up some small stones that peppered the grass, and tossed them into the lake. It reminded me of all the times Lucian and I had gone to the lake near the academy to skip stones. Thinking about how frustrated he'd always get because I was better than he was made me smile. He tried to hide it, but I could tell in the way his forehead would furrow, and his eyes crinkled when he was about to fling the stone.

Did he skip stones with Cassandra now? I didn't think so, she didn't seem like the tossing rocks type of girl.

It was so strange to think about his life without me in it, without ever meeting me. I considered how many things were the same; like having the same friends and being good at the same things—hand to hand combat for example. Then, there were the things that were different. They all still had red wings, so they never ascended to being demigods. That made me wonder if the big battle to overcome Zeus had ever happened. Revana was still alive, so that was a big possibility. Maybe Lucian was living in a timeline where Zeus didn't betray everyone, or maybe no one had found out about it yet.

Was he happy without me? He'd definitely looked happy. I couldn't remember a moment when he'd looked that relaxed and joyous around me. Maybe I wasn't any good for him, and instead, I was making his life miserable. That thought had crossed my mind even before being snapped out of existence and sent to the meadows.

Once I got back, that was something to consider. I was going to have to do a re-examination of our relationship. Whether it was good for either one of us. Maybe I needed to really let him go, like I needed to do with Hades.

While I waited, I thought about the Goddess of Witchcraft. She was an enigma. Both scary as hell, and kind and compassionate. Not like the woman Lucian had described. I didn't know what to expect when she had first found me and brought me to her cave, though she proceeded to try and eat me. In the past, she certainly hadn't been a friend, but that was how I was starting to think of her. She'd saved me now a few times and if that wasn't a friend, I didn't know what was.

She returned not long after, sat beside me, and we shared the berries she'd collected in the pouch of her skirt. It was nothing compared to the hearty meals I'd eaten at the academy, or shared with Hades in his hall, but at least it was something. Starving in a place like this would be horrific.

After we finished the berries, and watched over the water, I spied a ripple in the middle of the lake. At first, I thought maybe my eyes were just dry and sore, rippling from the grit in them, but then I saw it again. A bigger wave this time.

"Look. I see something." Pointing, I got to my feet, and edged closer to the water lapping onto the shore to get a better look. Hecate joined me and we both squinted over the gray mist.

Holding my breath, I watched and waited. More rippling spread, and a wave of water shot up over my boots. There was definitely something big moving around below the surface. We didn't have to wait long. A reptilian-like head with rows of webbed frills breached the lake, then another one, and another, until all nine heads stuck out of the water.

It was the hydra.

Grinning, I made a little whoop. "Thank the Gods."

Once the heads vanished, dipping back under the surface, it was enough for me to know that there was a way out of here. A way home. If the hydra could cross from this world to the next, then so could we. Without hesitation, I grabbed Hecate's hand, and started to walk into the lake.

She pulled back. "What are you doing?"

"Going home. All we have to do is swim down to where the hydra is, and find out how it came through."

"I don't have your water gifts. I won't be able to breathe that long underwater."

"Can you use a spell or something?"

Her brow furrowed. "I might be able to cast a protection spell around my head. Like a shield to keep the water out and the air in."

"Okay. Won't know until we try it."

Reluctantly nodding, she moved her hands in front of her in a complicated pattern. Soon, a green glow blossomed around her face. It grew and grew until it looked like a large balloon or helmet—her head in the center. Once done, she let me pull her into the water. I took in a deep breath, and kicked down into the lake. Hecate followed me down, but stopped to test her spell. After a few seconds of deep breathing, she gave me a thumbs up, and together, we dove as deep as we could go in search of the hydra and the portal back to the academy.

CHAPTER EIGHT

LUCIAN

*A*lone, I walked down the row of stalls in the stables, just outside the obstacle course and bow training field. Passing several unicorns and griffins that stomped their big feet in annoyance, I made my way to where the Pegasus was housed, and leaned over the half door.

"Hey beautiful."

Immediately walking over to me, Aella snorted, and butted my hand with her nose. Opening the stall, I came inside to brush her, and running my hand over the Pegasus's flank, I gave her a firm pat. It had been a few months since I'd taken her out for a ride, and she'd obviously missed it as well. Aella rewarded me by nuzzling my cheek.

"We'll go out soon, okay?"

When Aella butted me in the shoulder with her nose, I took that as a yes.

The night before I'd had another dream about the blue-haired warrior, and it made me want to come out to the stables. In the dream, "Blue" and I were training in the obstacle course with Artemis. Grabbing a bow and quiver of arrows, she ran for the stables while I watched from the sidelines.

When "Blue" came out again, she was riding Aethon—the biggest of the fire-breathing horses, and Ares's personal mount. If I'd told Ares about that girl riding Aethon in the dream, he would've laughed at me. No one had ever ridden his horse before. Yet, as she did, everyone in the crowd, including me, had been awestruck at her prowess and ability. "Blue" had completed the course in record time, beating Revana.

It also made me think about my own course training, and how Aella had allowed me to ride her into the challenge. I missed Aella's presence in turn, compelling me to come out to the stables to see her. I knew it had just been a dream, but something about it pricked at my memories, and the emotions I experienced during my training.

Once I finished brushing her, I fed Aella her favorite treat—a golden apple from one of the trees in the garden that Demeter tended. There was something so exhilarating about riding on the Pegasus as she soared though the air. I loved flying on my own, using my own wings, but sometimes it was just as powerful to be allowed to ride this beautiful winged horse. That Aella trusted me enough was an honor.

After leaving the stables, I wandered over to the practice field, to watch Artemis and Jasmine put the new recruits through their paces. Cassandra was one of those recruits, and I observed her as she picked up the bow, rapidly firing four arrows at the round targets down the field. Two of them hit the bullseye, the other two struck just outside.

As the others clapped and cheered at her achievement, she turned around and caught my gaze. Her nose crinkled as she smiled, and I grinned back. She looked so utterly surprised at her own skill and ability. That was one of the things I liked about Cassandra, her humbleness. It was very cute.

Then, her smile began to fade, and her arms went slack—the bow dropping from her grip. Just as it hit the ground, she listed to the side and also fell. As her body convulsed on the earth, I started to run toward her.

She was having a vision.

Others gathered around Cassandra, but did give her room. Artemis crouched next to her, gently holding her head so it wouldn't bounce on the hard-packed dirt. Standing over her, I just watched. There wasn't anything anyone could do, except make sure she didn't harm herself while she seized. I hated when she went through that as it just seemed so violent, even more so this time around, but it was part of who she was.

I'd witnessed her have three visions so far, and it never got easier. Although, this one seemed different. More powerful.

After another minute or two, Cassandra stopped convulsing. She lay still on the ground, her eyes closed. Once her eyelids finally fluttered open, she looked around at all the faces staring down at her with concern. Her gaze met mine and I offered her a little smile to let her know it was okay.

Artemis helped her sit up, and Jasmine handed her a bottle of water.

"I'm okay." Cassandra assured with a nod, and took a sip.

"Are you sure you're all right? You still look pale."

"I'm fine."

"It looked really intense this time."

Licking her lips, she grabbed my hand and Jasmine's, guiding us to the side, away from the others who had gone back to their training. "I have to tell you what I saw, and you have to believe me."

My brows wrinkled in confusion. "Okay. You're freaking me out a bit."

Exchanging a glance with me, Jasmine nodded. "Me too."

Yet, Cassandra's expression only sobered. "Someone is coming."

Jasmine gave her a look. "Who?"

"You don't know her in this life, but you did in another."

"You know I hate it when you talk in riddles," Jasmine grunted. "I can never figure them out."

Yet, I knew what she was talking about. "The blue-haired girl," I murmured. I knew instantly that was true.

Cassandra's fingers interlaced with mine, squeezing my hand. "Yes."

"What are you two talking about?" Jasmine

frowned at us both. "You don't mean the girl you had a dream about the other night?"

Sighing, I nodded.

"How can she be coming here? She's a dream person. She doesn't exist."

"I think she does exist," I replied, rubbing at my mouth. I was confused about the whole thing, but quietly sure Cassandra was telling the truth. "Cass and I both dreamt about her that night. And to be honest, it felt more like a memory than anything else."

"But how is that possible?" Jasmine pressed. "How can you have a memory of someone you've never met?"

"I don't know." I shrugged. "But haven't we seen a lot of things here at the academy that have been unbelievable?"

Calling Cassandra's attention, Jasmine focused on her. "What exactly did you see in your vision?"

"You, Lucian, Gina, Ren, and I were all standing on the shore of the lake at midday, waiting for something."

Jasmine's gaze lifted to the blue sky, the sun was just starting to reach its zenith. "You mean midday today?"

Cassandra nodded. "Yes, we need to get Gina and Ren, and we need to go to the lake right now."

"Why the lake?" Jasmine asked.

"I don't know exactly. My visions aren't always clear. Most times it's a feeling, more than anything else. A compulsion."

"And you feel compelled to go to the lake with all of us?"

Cassandra nodded, and I could see the panic and despair capturing her eyes. To have visions so intense must be terrifying.

"I don't get it." Jasmine shook her head. "Why is this girl so important?"

"I don't know," Cassandra confessed. "But we need to be there for her. We need to save her, because I think she will be the one to fix the world."

Taken aback by her words, Jasmine looked at me. "What do you think? Does this make any sense to you?"

I thought about the girl in my dreams. There was definitely something familiar about her. I didn't understand how I could know her and not remember her, but it seemed like it was true. Really strong emotions filled me both times I dreamt about her. It had to mean something. Maybe we were all suffering from some sort of mass amnesia.

"It doesn't make sense, but somehow, it feels true," I finally answered. "I think Cass is right. We need to get Gina and Ren and go to the lake."

"Okay," Jasmine conceded as she unfurled her wings. "This is crazy but heck, what isn't crazy about being at an academy for demigods, training to be in a Gods army? After a couple of years, it should all just be part of the course."

My red wings also spread out—the same hue as Jasmine's and the rest of my peers'. Yet, in that moment, I remembered that in my dream about the blue-haired warrior, my wings and the others' had been white—as if we had already ascended to demigod status. It was an interesting detail, I thought, one I hadn't really considered until now.

To get to the lake on time, we'd need to fly to the academy, find Gina and Ren, and fly to the lake. Holding Cassandra by the waist, since she didn't have her wings yet, I lifted us into the air. She immediately stiffened, and I knew she didn't like to fly. Really, I couldn't blame her; I probably wouldn't like it either if I had to be carried.

Our first stop was the gardens, where Georgina was most likely digging in the dirt, and talking to the plants that grew there. It was where she spent most days. Her attention shifted when we swooped in and landed by the fig trees. She walked over to us.

"You all look like you're on a mission." Her gaze went from my face, to Jasmine's, to Cassandra's. "What's up?"

"You need to come with us to the lake," I urged.

She made a face. "Why would I want to do that? I got work to do."

"It's hard to explain, but Cass had a vision just now, and we all need to go to the lake together."

"Why? What's supposed to happen?"

"They think the blue-haired girl from their dreams is going to be there or something," Jasmine said in a rush.

Georgina's eyebrows lifted. "Like a mermaid or something?"

"No, it's not like that." I threw up my hands in frustration. "Just, just come with us. Okay? It's important."

"Okay." , confused by my behavior.

"Do you know where Ren is?" I asked.

"The last time I saw him, he was heading to the forge. Something about Hephaistos making him a new trident or something."

We couldn't fly into the academy, so we went through the main doors, and toward the long, winding staircase that headed down into the belly of the building and the forge.

Before we could descend the stairs though, Aphrodite stepped in our way, pretty much blocking us. "Where are you all off to in such a hurry?"

Her question was basic and innocuous, but a shiver rushed down my back anyway. There was something in the way she looked at us, especially Cassandra, that rubbed me in the wrong way. In fact, a lot of things that the Goddess did and said bothered me, but I could never really pinpoint why. Her behavior was just off… wrong somehow.

"Hephaistos asked us to come help him with a project." The lie just rolled off my tongue. Luckily, none of the others looked at me strangely to give us away.

Aphrodite's gaze seemed to burrow into me, and I could tell she didn't believe me. Then she grinned, and it was her usually sardonic, humorless smile that dripped more venom than honey. "Have fun." Her hand waved us toward the stairs, as if giving us permission to use them.

And use them we did. We ran down the steps, and into the forge. Time was ticking.

When we found Ren, he was spinning his new

golden trident over his head. He stopped to show it to us. "Isn't it wicked?"

"It's great, but right now you need to come with us," I urged.

"Why, what's up?"

Georgina patted his arm. "Don't ask. Just accept your fate and come along quietly."

Thankfully he did. That was one thing I really liked about Ren, he was loyal, and didn't question too much. If there was something he could do for his friends, he always jumped to be first in line.

Leaving the school, we all took to the air, and I led the pack to the lake.

A thread of excitement coursed through me as we flew across the training fields, and spires of the academy. Something monumental was about to happen, I could feel it all the way to my bones. I didn't know who this blue-haired girl was, but I had to admit that I was vibrating with anticipation to meet her.

CHAPTER NINE

MELANY

*I*t didn't take long to realize how big and deep the lake was. It had to be to hide a twenty-five-foot, nine-headed, giant creature called a hydra.

I'd encountered the beast before, during the water trial in my first year at the academy. It had tried to eat my friend, Diego—well, maybe not eat him, but it was definitely playing around with its food—but Ren and I had rescued him. The hydra hadn't been happy about that, and it emerged from the water like a volcano. Ren and I did inadvertently win the trial, when we reached the beach on the huge wave the beast had made.

Kicking my legs swiftly, I kept going deeper. Hecate struggled a bit behind me, but so far, her spell was working. Her head remained emerged in the big bubble—much like one of those old timey diver's helmets. The water was murky, so it was hard to see, and I couldn't very well create a fire ball in the water for light.

I glanced over at Hecate. "We need light?" With my hands, I mimed not being able to distinguish anything.

She must've understood what I was babbling about, because her hands flicked around in the water, and a soft green glow formed in front of her. Nudging it forward, she sent it floating in front of us. It wasn't bright, but it was enough for me to see a few feet ahead of us.

After diving down another few feet, I finally spotted the spiked tail of the hydra. Careful not to get too close—I really didn't want it to turn around and eat us—we followed it down to the bottom of the lake.

When the hydra reached the rocky terrain, it started to walk along the edge, but it seemed like it was just taking a daytime stroll. Frustration filled me, and hope started to seep out of my pores. Maybe I had been wrong. Maybe there was no portal and Hecate and I were stuck in the meadows for the rest of eternity, slowly going mad with each passing day.

We continued to follow the hydra, but my lungs were starting to ache. I couldn't hold my breath forever. The longest I'd reached, back at the academy, was fifteen minutes—when Ren and I were playing around in the pool at the elemental training room—and I was sure we were nearing that time limit. Eventually, I would have to go back up to the surface to take in some oxygen, and then dive down again.

My attention shifted to Hecate, wondering if she could make me one of her air bubble heads. I was about to ask her, when the hydra started digging in the bottom.

After a few minutes of digging, a hole was created, a large gaping hole. Then, it did a nine-headed dive into it, kicking hard with its back legs. Incredulously, I watched as the huge beast disappeared into the sand, all that was left was his tail, which quickly got sucked into the crevice. It sort of looked like a pool of quicksand.

We swam down to get a closer look. It had to

have been a portal. There was no way the hydra, that was the size of a brachiosaurus dinosaur, could just disappear into a hole in the bottom of the lake. It wasn't a crab.

As my gaze connected with Hecate's, I pointed to the hole, which was slowly starting to refill with sand and rocks.

She shook her head and shrugged.

Glancing back to the hole, urgency filled me. It was now or never. We wouldn't get another chance.

I dove down into the burrow, kicking as hard as I could to squirm my way into the strange portal. As I sawm, I hoped Hecate had followed, but I couldn't worry about her right now. I was too busy trying not to get grit in my nose and mouth. That would be just my luck, to drown in a pool of quicksand while underwater.

For a few seconds—completely submersed in the sand—the granules in my hair, ears, and peppering my cheeks threatened to invade my nostrils and eyes, until I thought that was how I was going to die. I could feel my lungs being crushed while the air was expelled out of me. I'd already lost the chance to swim back to the surface to get more air. I lost any chance to do anything but keep digging through the portal.

I wasn't even sure I could get out anymore.

The thought of never seeing Lucian and my friends again kept me pushing forward. I had to get back home to them. Even if they didn't remember me, I wanted—needed—to see them again. Touch them, hug them, laugh with them. Without them, I would be nothing.

Without them in my life, it wouldn't be worth living.

With that in my mind, I scrambled harder through the silt, my lungs nearly bursting. Black spots started to dance around in my vision, I was going to pass out. My head didn't feel attached to my body. My arms were getting weaker by the second, and I couldn't move my right one anymore.

I was done. I couldn't do it.

Movement abruptly came from behind me; someone was pushing on my legs and back. Pushing me to keep going. Gathering the last of my strength, I pushed my right arm forward through the muck, wriggled my back end, and kicked with my legs as hard as I could...

I went through it.

Cold, dark water suddenly surrounded me again, sucking me out of the hole in the sandy bottom. I nearly opened my mouth to take in much needed air, but I stopped myself before I swallowed a lung-full of liquid.

Glancing at my feet, I found Hecate emerging from the quicksand portal, and with the small amount of energy I had, I grabbed her hand, yanking her out through the last little bit. I wanted to hug her tightly, knowing she'd been the one to push me through at the end, but we needed to swim like mad to the top of this lake before I drowned.

I had no oxygen left.

At least I hoped it was the lake at the academy. Right now, I didn't have any way of truly knowing. All I knew was that I needed to breathe before my lungs exploded.

Pulling from whatever energy was left in me, I urgently kicked, and swam up toward the surface—trying hard not let desperation or panic sink its claws on me. Moving my body like a porpoise, I shimmied back and forth through the water. I could see the top of the lake now, about twenty feet above us. Sunlight pierced the surface, its rays were beacons of hope. I clung to those, since there had been no sun in the meadows. It had to have meant we made it across the portal to the academy. The sight of the beams of light caused adrenaline to surge through my body, and I shot straight up like an arrow.

The closer we got the more details I could distinguish. Some thrashing came from the water above—someone else was in the lake. Looking for us maybe? Could it be Lucian. Jasmine, or Georgina? I didn't know why that crossed my mind. There was no reason for them to look for me, especially since when I saw them last, in my dream, they didn't even know I existed.

Still, the sight of someone else gave me even more hope.

Lungs burning, and my vision darkening from lack of air, I raised my hand, reaching for someone to grab me. Anyone. It didn't matter. I just needed to feel the touch of another person from my past. It would be a confirmation that I was still real. That I truly existed.

Instead of a helping hand, a shockwave reached me. I didn't see the hydra's tail swinging toward me until it was too late.

Its powerful spiked ball smacked me across the midsection, sending me spiraling into the deep lake once again. Hecate spun the other way.

Blinding pain coursed through my body from the blow, and my mouth opened in a half gasp, half scream, unable to hold my breath any longer. Blood swirled up in front of my face as cold water rushed into my weak lungs. It was my blood. That much I knew, even without having to touch the wound in my side.

Trying not to drown, I thrashed about... but it was too late.

I was already dead.

CHAPTER TEN

LUCIAN

*O*ne by one we landed on the shore of the lake. The sun was reaching the zenith in the sky, and its beams pierced the veil of the tall oak trees, spearing the calm surface of the water. It made the lake sparkle like a pool of diamonds.

That was one of my favorite places, and I went often since arriving at the academy a couple of years ago. It was a space of peace and calm for me. I often found myself there alone, sitting by the shore to think. Sometimes, I would skip rocks along the water's surface, always trying to get it past four skips as if I was competing with someone else.

Standing next to me, Jasmine looked around us. "What are we doing here, exactly?"

Cassandra stepped right to the edge of the lake, intently examining the surface.

"For what?" Jasmine asked, walking closer to Cassandra. "I know your visions usually come true, but this just seems so, I don't know, weird."

She shrugged. "I know, and I can't explain it, but we are supposed to be here right now."

Feeling strangely anxious, I stood on Cassandra's other side, taking her hand in mine. "I believe you, Cass."

"I didn't say I didn't believe her." Jasmine frowned at me. "It's just strange, that's all."

Georgina and Ren also came up to stand by the shore. "How long do we wait?" Georgina asked.

Cassandra's gaze lifted to the sky, then went back to the lake. "Not long."

Not sure what to expect, we all went back to glancing at the still surface.

Waiting...

The water started to ripple the next moment. There was no wind or anything in sight, so it had to be coming from underneath it.

Cassandra squeezed my hand, and let go. "Get ready. You're going to need to move fast."

Before I could question what she meant, bubbles rose in the middle of the lake, and waves surged onto the shore, lapping at our shoes.

"It's the hydra," Jasmine mumbled, confused. "I thought we were waiting for the blue-haired girl to show up."

"She followed it here from *nowhere*. You have to save her from it."

Her stern gaze connected with mine, and I swallowed, accepting the truth in her words.

It seemed impossible, but I believed she was right. Somehow, I felt it deep down in my bones, as if that truth was a part of me. A different me. It didn't completely make sense in my mind, but sometimes you just had to take a leap of faith and accept that destiny had a path just for you.

And with that leap of faith in my mind, I dove into the water.

At first, I couldn't really see anything. It was dark and murky under the surface, but as I neared the center of the lake, the water churned with bubbles as something thrashed in it. I swam through the foam, and immediately came up behind the hydra. It was busy circling something. Its heads all curved inwards, keeping nine sets of eyes on whatever posed a threat.

I didn't know what that could be, considering the size and fierceness of the beast, but something had it riled up. Careful not to catch the hydra's attention, I swam a little further, and that was the moment I saw the threat. Still, she didn't appear to be dangerous at all, in fact, she looked like she was in serious trouble by the sight of all the blood floating around her.

It was the girl with blue hair.

"Blue..."

Strangely, my chest heavily constricted at the sight of her injured. I was about to hurry over to her but something else caught my attention. Hecate, the Goddess of Witchcraft, floated nearby. What was she doing here? I'd hadn't seen her since the battle with the typhon, and what was she doing here with the blue-haired girl. There was a green glow around her head like a globe. She too was struggling in the water, and the hydra was aiming for her next.

I dove toward her, kicking my legs as hard and fast as I could. Her eyes widened in surprise when she saw me, and I grabbed her hand, yanking her out of the hydra's way. Swimming up with her swiftly, we breached the surface.

"Come get her," I motioned for Jasmine to help. "I need to go back down!"

"Do you need help?" Ren shouted.

"Yes!"

Trident still in hand, Ren immediately dove into the water, heading toward me. I was happy to have him join me; he was a stronger and faster swimmer than I was. Ren moved through the water like he was born in it. He should've been an Atlantean instead of a demigod. Plus, he had a weapon with him. A weapon I had a feeling we were going to need.

When he reached me, I pointed to the girl still floating in a pool of crimson. She hadn't moved much, but I knew she was alive. She had to be. Cassandra's visions were always right.

The hydra circled her again, and I had a sense that this time it was going to move in for the kill.

Tapping me on the shoulder, Ren pointed at the hydra, then from me to the girl, indicating he was going to distract the hydra while I got to her. At least I hoped that was what he said. Either way, Ren didn't wait, and immediately dolphin-swam toward the hydra's nine heads.

It didn't take long before the hydra noticed Ren coming at it, and it opened a few mouths to roar at

him. The sound waves surged through the water
and knocked me back a few feet. Swiftly, I regained
my senses, shooting like an arrow toward the girl,
while Ren started to poke the beast's heads with his
shiny new golden trident.

When I reached her, I wasn't sure if she was
alive, she was so limp and unresponsive. I wrapped
an arm around her waist, and started swimming
back with her. I willed her eyelids to open and focus
on me, to give me some indication that she was
going to make it, but she remained unconscious and
half-drowned in my arms.

My chest started to ache, as my lungs burned
for air, despite the fact that I could hold my breath
longer than regular people. I didn't know how this
girl could still be alive. She had to have been in the
water for a long time.

After a few more minutes, I started to struggle,
carrying her and getting us to the top. I reached
deep into my water power that swirled around
inside me and found the strength to kick harder. I
could see the sparkling surface of the lake. We were
almost there.

Ren suddenly shot by me in a panic. "Go!" He
shouted in the water. "It's coming!"

After I glanced over my shoulder, I really wish I

hadn't. The hydra was torpedoing right for us, every mouth open, displaying rows of razor-sharp teeth.

Trying to propel us higher and faster, I turned back, weaving my arm through the lake. The water above us suddenly started to swirl, like a whirlpool. Ren must have made us a whirlpool portal. It grew bigger and bigger, until it surrounded all three of us. Then we shot through it like a reverse slide.

When we breached the surface, I gasped for air, worry burning through me because she couldn't do the same. Her head fell back while in my hold, unconscious, and liquid dribbled out of her mouth.

I pushed her up and swam toward the shore. About a few feet out, Jasmine got in, taking the girl from me. She dragged her onto the sand while Ren and I followed behind her. We made it just in time, before the hydra broke through, jaws snapping and roaring in frustration.

Jasmine settled the blue-haired girl onto her side, but she still didn't move. "I think she's dead."

Hecate crawled over to the girl's side. "She's not dead. She didn't come all this way to die."

Avoiding Hecate's gaze, which was dark and intense, and sent unusual images flashing in my mind. One in particular of her sucking out my blood sent a shiver of dread down my body. I put my attention back onto the blue-haired girl.

Gently, my fingers settled along the girl's neck to feel her pulse. It was there, but really faint. Concerned, I lifted her shirt a little to check the wound along her side. She had punctures in her flesh, fresh blood slowly oozed out of it. She needed healing but first she needed to breathe.

"Do you know her?" Jasmine asked, her brow crinkled as she stared down at us. "I feel like I've seen her before."

I didn't answer, focusing on tilting the girl's head back and pinching her nose closed; I prepared to do CPR. I had to get her breathing. I couldn't lose her... *again?*

The strange thought made me shake my head to concentrate, and I blew into her mouth once more, resuming compressions. I was about to get more air into her, when she began to cough. Bubbles of water sputtered out of her mouth, and I turned her onto her side so she could get it all out.

After she coughed up a storm, spewing more water out, she inhaled long and deep, finally catching her breath. The blue-haired girl rolled onto her back, and blinked up at me. I could tell she was trying to focus and having trouble.

"Gina, can you heal her?" I asked.

Georgina crouched down and inspected the injuries. "They don't look deep." She placed both p onto the girl's torso, closed her eyes, and concentrated. Not as good a healer as Chiron, Georgina still had mad skills. Her healing ability stemmed from her affinity to the earth and to nature. The human body was part of that cycle.

After a few minutes, Georgina lifted her palms. The skin along the wounds had knitted back together and no longer bled. She'd still need some bandages, but for now, she wouldn't bleed to death.

Carefully rolling her onto her back, I swept blue strands of hair out of her face. The color had drained from her skin, and it made the scars along her cheek even darker, angrier. Despite that though, she was stunning.

Finally, she seemed to stabilize and looked at me. Really looked at me.

"Gods, I never thought I'd see you again."

Brows scrunching together, I looked up at the others, they all had similar confused expression on their faces.

Her gaze went to Jasmine, Georgina, and Ren as she sat up, then returned to me. "You better remember who I am, or I'm going to be even more pissed at Nyx for snapping me into oblivion."

I didn't know what to say to her. I could see the pain on her face, the longing in her eyes. She definitely was the girl from my dreams, but other than that, I couldn't acknowledge that I truly knew her.

That would be a lie. I thought. My head started to hurt from the puzzlement of the entire situation.

Helped by the Witch Goddess, the girl got to her feet. "Hecate, help me out here. I thought coming back from the Meadows would break the goddess' spell."

"I don't know why they still don't remember."

"This is bullshit!" She threw her hands in the air. "I didn't fight my way back to the academy, not to be remembered by my own boyfriend and my best friends."

"Boyfriend?" Jasmine snorted.

The blue-haired girl moved so suddenly, that I didn't register it until she was right in front of me. My cheek rippled with force when her hand connected with it. "Snap out of it!"

"What the hell?" I rubbed at my stinging skin from her slap.

"Remember me!" Gripping the front of my shirt in her hand, she pulled me to her.

Her soft lips crashed against mine, and sparks literally flew from between them. It kind of felt like I was being electrocuted.

For just a second, I struggled with the feeling, until something warm and inviting surged through me. I stopped fighting it.

Clutching her waist, I kissed her back. I couldn't help myself. She felt so right in my arms.

When I pulled away, I just stared at her, wide-eyed and stunned as memories flooded into me like a volcano eruption.

When I first saw her in the water at pier six.

Heracles' hand to hand combat class as we sparred together.

Dancing with her during the welcome party that Dionysus had prepared.

Flying class, and the moment she sprouted gorgeous black wings instead of red.

Our first kiss…

The distress that burned my insides when Zeus electrocuted her.

The fear for her life that plagued me when she disappeared.

Being jealous when she returned with Hades.

Having sex with her for the first time on the shore of this very lake.

Falling in love...

Reality slammed into me, and I shook my head clear while she hugged each of our friends. Their expressions changed as one by one memories of her filled them. Knowing exactly how they were feeling, I watched, until I couldn't feel anything anymore but pure, unbridled joy to see Melany again.

"Blue, where the hell have you been?"

Facing me again she grinned, relieved. "I'm so happy to hear you ask me that question."

CHAPTER ELEVEN

MELANY

*I*n amazement, I watched as the timeline fixed itself right in front of my eyes.

Lucian's wings, and the others', which lay folded on their backs, turned from red to white. Jasmine's hair grew long again, falling in big dark curls past her shoulders. Georgina's metal arm vanished, leaving her with half an arm to her elbow like I remembered, and the golden trident Ren had been holding disappeared.

Other things changed too, but I couldn't see them, I just felt them flow through me and the others like an electrical energy. I imagined that energy was also altering their memories. Soon after, they were all staring at me, blinking, with looks of confusion and bewilderment. It was as if they all just suddenly awoke. In a way, I supposed that was exactly what happened.

Lucian was the first one to snap out of it. He came to me and pulled me into his arms. "Gods, Blue. Where the hell have you been?"

I sighed into his chest. "You have no idea how good it is to hear you call me Blue."

"Why wouldn't I?" His confusion grew when he looked down, finally noticing my injury, and he pulled back. "What happened?"

"Um, I was nearly gored by the hydra."

His brow furrowed. "The hydra? Where was it?"

"In the lake. You don't remember fighting it off, pulling me out of the water, and giving me mouth to mouth to save me?"

Slowly, he shook his head, looking at me like I was insane.

I peeked over to Hecate, who had yet to say or do anything. She actually looked like she was in shock. "He doesn't remember not remembering me?" I asked her.

"For them, nothing has changed. The past is

still the past they remember. You and I are the only ones who know what we know. I imagine that to them, we just walked out of the water."

That was crazy. My mind was actually blown.

Turning, I glanced at Cassandra. She stood kind of away from everyone, nervously rubbing her arms. She met my gaze briefly, but dropped it to the ground. Did she still remember? Did she see me now like I'd stolen her boyfriend? I felt bad for her if that was the case. I remembered how I felt seeing her with Lucian, with him having no memory of me at all.

Leaving the others, I walked over to her. "Thank you for saving us."

"I didn't do anything."

"You got everyone here, didn't you, with your vision?" It all must've been so strange for her, considering she had the same vision in this timeline and the other one.

Cassandra nodded.

"Then you saved my life." Grabbing her shoulders, I hugged her, but she became as stiff as a board in my arms. "Do you remember everything?" I whispered against her ear.

Once she leaned away and looked me in the

eyes, I knew the answer. "Yes," she murmured anyway, her voice barely audible.

I nodded. "I'm sorry."

"Okay, what is going on?" Lucian's frown deepened, and he gestured to Cassandra and me. "What are you sorry about?"

"That's between Cassandra and I."

"Okay… Then what are you and Hecate talking about? And besides, how did the two of you end up in the lake together?"

Sighing, I shook my head. "I don't even know where to begin, or how to explain."

"Start with, where you've been for the past week." Jasmine's hand landed on her hip, and she gave me that annoyed look of hers.

"Shit, I've been gone that long?"

"Yeah," they all said in unison.

"Well, let's see," I started, "it all began when Tisiphone ambushed me in the hall, and took me to the Temple of Night to talk to Nyx about her son Thanatos."

"You really went to the sky realm?" Georgina asked, her eyes wide with interest.

"Yeah. It was pretty cool too, until that bitch, Nyx, snapped me into oblivion."

Everyone just looked at me funny.

"Okay, this story is going to need some ice cream. And chocolate. And pancakes. I'm starving." A shiver rushed over me as a cool wind blew over my wet clothes and skin. "But first we all need to dry off."

Concentrating on the fire within, I dried my clothes. When I was done, my hands glowed red. I didn't form any flames as I didn't want to light anyone on fire. I dried Lucian and Ren, but when I went over to Jasmine, whose pants had only gotten wet, I noticed she was already dry.

"How did you do that?" I asked.

Frowning, she shook her head, while touching her pants. "I don't know."

"Make a fire ball," I demanded.

"I can't, remember? I don't have my fire powers anymore."

"Try it."

"Fine."

As Jasmine held out her hands, her eyes closed. Wrinkles gathered on her face, scrunched up in concentration, and I could see the frustration growing there. Yet, the next second, a few flames ignited from her fingertips. Surprised, her eyes sprung open and she stared down at her hands.

Fire grew higher and brighter in her palms,

until she had a good-sized orange globe. Laughter escaped her. "I never thought I'd be able to do that again!"

Giddy with excitement, I whirled around to face Lucian. "Make a lightning bolt."

Taking a deep breath, he clapped his hands together, and sparks immediately shot out. A grin tilted his lips, and when he pulled his palms apart, a spear of white lightning formed between them.

Georgina instantly dropped to the ground, placing her hand onto the dirt. Moments later, a brilliant green vine curled out of the earth, winding its way around her wrist lovingly. Tears sprung in her eyes.

With a wild whoop, Ren turned and dove into the lake, disappearing from view.

"Why do we have our powers back?" Lucian asked, stunned.

"I don't know." Gauging my body, I realized I didn't feel any different. I could still sense all the energy that each of my friends had given me within my core. To check, I called all of the power forward, until I had fire licking my hands and arms. A waterspout spun in front of me, while vines grew around my feet, and lightning cracked the sky above us. My shadows, the one power that innately belonged to me, the one that I was born with, hovered around on the ground waiting for my command.

I snuffed everything out, then turned to look at Hecate. "Any ideas?"

Her shoulders lifted and fell as she shrugged. "It's possible the two realities have intertwined."

"Who runs the academy?" I asked Lucian.

"What?" A nervous laugh escaped him. "What kind of question is that?"

"Just answer it, please."

He frowned but answered, "Prometheus."

I let out the breath I didn't realize I was holding in. "Thank the Gods. What about Aphrodite and Ares, are they still in Tartarus?"

He nodded.

"Okay, at least that hasn't changed." For a moment, I thought of asking about Hades, but I promised myself while in the meadows that I would let that hope go, so I refrained from it. I figured I'd find that out on my own anyway.

Ren suddenly came flying out of the water, laughing, and startling all of us on shore. He landed, shaking off his body just like a dog after a bath. "You have no idea how good that felt!"

With the way Jasmine, Georgina, and Lucian

shared in his joy, I thought they did know all too well, and I was beyond relieved that they'd regained their powers. For months I'd been carrying around this guilt in my gut, and it weighed on me every day. Now, I could let that go as well.

"Okay, let's head back to the academy. There's much to tell you and I desperately need pancakes, lots of whipped cream, and chocolate."

My attention shifted to Hecate again. I hated seeing her so broken. "You're coming with us, right?"

"I suppose, as I have nowhere else to go."

"I'll make sure Prometheus finds you a place in the school," I promised. In my opinion, she'd be a fantastic addition to the professors. The witch goddess could teach the recruits about magic, and when they didn't behave or mouth off to her, she could twist her head like The Exorcist and let her "other" personalities scare the crap out of them into behaving.

As easy as breathing, I pulled at the darkness around us, gathering the shadows until I encased all seven of us. It would be a lot faster than flying. Besides, Cassandra and Hecate didn't have wings, and I was much too tired from nearly drowning to carry anyone.

I also needed to see Chiron so he could patch me up properly. It was still freaking me out that Lucian and the others didn't remember what actually happened in the lake, to get me and Hecate here. I wasn't sure I'd ever be able to rectify it in my mind. Just like I knew that when I told them what happened, and what I'd seen in their reality without me, they weren't going to be able to wrap their minds around it.

Picturing the dining hall, I pulled all of us through the shadows and into the room. Thankfully, it was empty, so I wouldn't have to deal with a bunch of questions from other people, and I could just concentrate on stuffing my face full of food and healing. And sleep, glorious, lovely sleep. I was going to sleep for a few days.

Once we were through, I asked Lucian to make me a plate while I took Hecate to see Chiron, and so I could get a bandage. He pressed a quick kiss to my forehead, and I took the witch through the shadows to the infirmary. When we stepped out, Chiron was there, as if waiting for us to show.

"Why do I get the feeling that you knew we were coming?"

"Apollo stopped by and told me that you'd show

up sometime today." His gaze fell to my blood-stained shirt. "Let's have a look."

Complying, I lifted my shirt, and as quick and efficient as ever, he covered my wound with some stinking salve, then bandaged me up. When he was done, he looked at Hecate, but she just stared right through him. I was worried that she would never be normal again. Or as normal as a witch with three entities living inside of her could be.

Gently, he took her arm. "C'mon, love, let's get you cleaned up. I'll fix you up with a room, and some tea to help you sleep."

"Can you talk to Prometheus about getting her a teaching gig?"

He looked at me strangely but nodded.

Confident in Chiron's abilities, I stepped back into the shadows, and returned to the dining hall. Everyone was sitting at our table, waiting for me, so I sat down in front of the plate stacked with pancakes, fruit, whipped cream, and chocolate sauce drizzled all over it. Just the way I liked it. In that moment, I felt tears stinging my eyes. Lucian remembered what I liked. I was home.

As I wolfed down the food, I proceeded to tell them about my conversation with death, and how I ended up in Asphodel Meadows with Hecate.

Deliberately, I left out the parts about Hecate trying to eat me, and my thoughts that she may have eaten other people. She'd been through enough. She needed to heal as well as I did.

"So, you think Aphrodite is messing around with the Fates in order to resurrect Zeus?" Jasmine asked.

I nodded. "It would make sense. She's had the most to lose with Zeus gone. And she is a master at revenge."

"And when you were in the meadows, you were wiped out of our memories?" Georgina plucked a ripe strawberry from my plate and popped it into her mouth.

"Not only your memories, but the entire string of reality. I didn't exist at all."

Jasmine shook her head. "Wow. That's... I can't even imagine that. Was I still with Mia in that reality?"

"As far as I saw, yes."

"What else was different?" Lucian asked.

Discreetly, I glanced over at Cassandra. She was watching the whole thing with a sad expression on her face. I wouldn't tell them about her and Lucian. I didn't want to hurt her, and make things awkward for Lucian.

"Lots of things. The most jarring was that Zeus was still around, and we didn't have the big war with him in Pecunia. You guys had just fought the typhon."

Lucian rubbed at his face. "That just doesn't seem possible. Especially that we don't remember it that way."

"Yeah, as you can imagine, it was a bit disconcerting to see you—all of you—just living your lives without ever knowing me. Kind of makes a person feel pretty insignificant."

Lucian's arm slung around me, and he pulled me close. "You will never be insignificant."

I gave him a small smile.

"So, you went through all of that to talk to Thanatos," Jasmine added. "Now, what's the plan? Because if I know you, you have a plan to fix all of this. You wouldn't be you, if you didn't want to go charging into danger, risking your life and limb."

Finishing the last of the food on my plate, I set the fork down. "The plan is to go to Tartarus, find Aphrodite, and make her tell me how to get to the Cave of Memory. I need to talk to the Fates, and find out what the hell is going on."

CHAPTER TWELVE

MELANY

"Υου just got back, and you're already planning on leaving again?" Lucian shook his head, concern gleaming in his eyes.

"I plan on sleeping first."

Jasmine gave me a look. "You're not going on your own this time, Mel. We are going with you. I'm getting tired of you disappearing without a trace. One time it will be for good, and I won't be able to handle that."

"Honestly, I was hoping you would say that," I

admitted with a chuckle. "Because I have no idea how to get into Tartarus."

"I'm pretty sure Prometheus is the only one with a key," Lucian added.

"Then we'll have to find a way to steal the key."

Ren snorted. "I'd love to just have one year at the academy where we aren't facing grave danger and doing something we shouldn't be doing. Like, can't we just be cool professors and revel in all the perks?"

I patted him on the shoulder. "Yeah, but where would the fun be in that?"

"And what perks are you getting?" Jasmine asked.

Yet, not everyone looked enthused about the possibility of another dangerous adventure. Georgina had yet to say anything. She wouldn't even meet my gaze.

"Gina?" I reached across the table to touch her hand. "What's going on?"

"I was kind of hoping that when I got my earth powers again, my arm would somehow magically grow back." She shook her head. "It was a stupid thing to assume."

My chest constricted with her words. "I may not

be able to help you grow your arm back, but I do have the next best thing."

Giving me a weird look, she scrunched her nose. "I'm almost scared to ask."

After we finished eating, I led everyone down the stone stairs to the forge. If I'd been gone over a week, that should've been enough time for Hephaistos to make the mechanical arm that I'd commissioned for Georgina. Cassandra tried to get out of it, saying she didn't belong, but I grabbed her arm and told her she was one of us now, and she needed to accept it whether she liked it or not.

That made Jasmine snort laugh.

When we stepped through the open metal door, voices carried down from one of the upper platforms and we halted, pressing our backs against one of the large stone walls near the lower forge.

"You are crazy to think I have any control over her whatsoever." Hephaistos's voice seemed stressed, and I wondered which "her" he was talking about.

"Well, you need to do something before she destroys it all." The second voice was a huge surprise. It belonged to Hera, the Goddess of the Stars, and Zeus's long-suffering wife.

Now I was really curious as to who the "her"

they were discussing was. Was it Aphrodite? Was it me? Also, what was the "it" in the equation? The plot to resurrect Zeus? Fixing fate and time?

"And do it before I do."

"I don't do well with threats, Hera. They make my skin itchy."

"Who do you think she's talking about?" I whispered, glancing at the others.

"Could be anyone," Lucian responded.

I didn't think so. I thought there were only a couple of people Hera could be asking Hephaistos to contain. A couple of people who were connected to him. There weren't many who could claim that.

A few seconds later, Hera—resplendent in her usual dark blue gown and crown affixed to her mass of curly hair—appeared at the top of the stone steps leading down from the platform. We all pressed deeper into the shadows along the wall, and I pulled the darkness around us, so we were invisible.

The Goddess came down the steps, passed by us and left the forge. When she was gone, we emerged from the shadows and climbed up to where Hephaistos toiled in the fire of his main forge.

Unsure if we should mention Hera's visit, and

after a quick glance to the others, I approached him. "Hey, Heph."

His usual scowl was etched in his granite face when he turned. He sighed, obviously pissed at having been interrupted again. "What do you want? Can't you see I'm busy!"

"Came to see if you had that thing done that I wanted you to make?"

"Right." Setting the long pliers he'd been holding onto the stone table, he gestured for us to follow him down the other stone steps, to where he stored all the amazing things he made—like the shadowboxes. It didn't matter how many times I'd come down to the forge and seen the work he did, I was always amazed by his delicate craftsmanship.

We gathered around his workbench as he went to the shelves and took down the brass and silver looking metal arm he'd made for Georgina. Her eyes grew as wide as saucers when Hephaistos approached her with it.

"Melany thought that you could do with a little extra."

Her big eyes watered when she looked at me, so I came over to her side, hugging her close. "You're going to look so badass with this thing."

Hephaistos fitted it over the stump at her elbow,

swinging a strap over her shoulder to keep it in place. He tightened the strap to make sure if fit snugly but wasn't too uncomfortable for her. "How does that feel?"

Firelight reflected on the metal as she lifted her new arm, getting a sense of it. "It feels... weird, but good."

"You should be able to move and use your fingers with the electrical impulses that run through your arm. The bronze tubes that are fitted to your elbow will be able to pick up those signals and shoot them down to your fingers." Setting his hand over hers, he bent the rigid digits toward her the palm. "Now, try and straighten them."

Georgina's brow furrowed as she concentrated on moving the bronze contraption. Her pinky finger twitched, but that was all. Shoulders dropping, she sighed in frustration. "I can't do it."

I squeezed her good shoulder. "It's going to take time and practice, Gina. Just remember that metal is part of the earth. You can move boulders across a field, I've seen you do it, so I know you can do this."

She nodded to me, then put her attention back onto her arm. Concentrating on the manufactured hand, she frowned, her brow creasing. I so wanted to push my own power into her, but I knew that wouldn't help her. She needed to do it on her own.

Her face scrunched up fully, until all her fingers straightened, and she grinned.

Everyone cheered and Jasmine patted her on the back. "I knew you could do it. You're a super-hero now."

"Well, I don't know about that, but it'll be nice to be able to use both my hands to tend to the garden."

Laughter escaped me. Here she was, with this very cool, very powerful new metallic arm, and all she wanted to do with it was play in the dirt and grow some plants and flowers. Other people would've been talking about how they could crush skulls, break bones, or punch their way through a wall—okay, maybe that wasn't other people, that was just me—and Georgina just wanted to be able to caress one of the trees in the garden.

"I bet your arm will come in handy when we get to Tartarus," Ren quipped.

As the words came out of his mouth, I grimaced. "Ren, shut up."

Hephaistos's head whipped around and he glared at me. "Tartarus? Why the hell would you be going there?"

"To talk to Aphrodite," I explained. "She knows how to get to the Cave of Memory."

"And who told you that?"

"Thanatos." I grimaced again.

Hephaistos's glare got fiercer and more intimidating. The others visibly shrunk but I was used to his surliness.

"You can't always believe what you hear."

"So, Aphrodite didn't go to the Fates to beg for Paris's life during the Trojan War?"

The look on his face darkened. I guessed I must've hit a sore spot. Maybe Ares wasn't the first or only person she had used to cheat on him. It still baffled me how he could've kept being married to her. I didn't profess to the understand the Gods, but their marriage was one of the most perplexing things of all.

"Girl, what are you getting yourself and your friends into? You need to leave well enough alone for your own good."

"Well, I've already been snapped into oblivion by the Goddess of the Night and survived. So, I figure there isn't too much else that could be as bad."

He smirked. "You say that because you've never been to Tartarus."

"Have you?"

He didn't respond. Which usually meant an affirmative answer.

"How do we get there?" I asked. "Is Prometheus the only one with a key? Is there another way in?"

With a grunt, he walked, well limped, away from the workbench, and back to the stone staircase leading back up to the highest platform and the main forge. "You can all leave now. You got what you came here for."

Except, I couldn't let it go. It was too important. Life, fate, death, it was all on the line right now. "You can't walk away from this. You know something bad is happening, and it's not just about the shadowboxes and the lack of new recruits."

He didn't stop, so I continued to walk after him.

"Time itself is being unraveled. I've seen it when I was in Asphodel Meadows. The dead aren't dying, Hephaistos, and I'm certain someone is trying to find the Fates so they can resurrect Zeus."

Hephaistos's steps halted that time, and I slammed into his back with an audible oomph. Slowly, he turned to glower down at me. "You need to watch yourself, girl. Not everyone wants to see you succeed."

"You mean, Hera? Was she here to warn you about me? If so, why?"

Sighing, he scrubbed his big hands over his stone-like face. "Gods, you ask so many questions you make my head hurt."

"Then help me, and I'll go away. Wouldn't that be nice? Not to have me badgering you all the time?" I smiled sweetly at him.

He shook his head. "Tartarus is as far below Hades's Hall, as Olympus is above the Earth. In other words, it's a really, really, really long way down."

"Okay, so how do we get there? Is there a tunnel, or a path, or what?"

"The best way to get there, is to ask someone who's escaped."

More questions popped into my head. So many questions. I opened my mouth again to ask, but he put his big hand up to stop me. I could see in his face that he was so done with me.

"I'm tired, and I have a headache. Go away." Turning around, he left.

I let him go… this time.

When I returned to the others, they were all gathered around Georgina, watching what she could do with her new appendage.

Lucian looked up at me. "Did you get the answers you wanted?"

"I guess." . "Who do we know who was once in Tartarus?"

His brow wrinkled as he frowned, then I saw the answer come to him, and he didn't look very happy. I had a feeling I wasn't going to like what he was going to say.

CHAPTER THIRTEEN

MELANY

$\mathcal{I}$t took a bit to needle the answer out of Lucian, but once I did, I wasn't sure I was prepared for it. I mean, how did I prepare to meet the person who may have been responsible for my adoptive mother's—Sophie's death?

Since we had powers that could aid us when dealing with the giants, I suggested to the others that Jasmine, Georgina, and I would go to the stone castle in the mountains to face the cyclopes. While we were gone, the others would have to cover for us. It would be easy to cover for me, because it was usual for me to just disappear for days at a time without telling anyone.

For Lucian, however, it would be more difficult. He was looked upon as the responsible one. Disappearing without word would be out of character for him. So, I gave him, Ren, and Cassandra the task of figuring out how to get the key from Prometheus, which was likely going to be harder than just talking to a couple of Titans.

We traveled through the shadows, which seemed to be working better since returning from Asphodel Meadows. I didn't know exactly why. It was as perplexing as why Lucian, Jasmine, Georgina and Ren had all gotten their powers back, while I continued to possess them as well. Hecate suspected something about our timelines converging. Maybe that was it.

It didn't take long through the shadow ways—ten minutes maximum—before we stepped out into sunshine, entering the parking lot at the base of the famous Mount Olympus and the trail leading up to it. Luckily, there were only a few cars parked nearby, and no one around to see us just appear out of thin air. It wasn't that our existence was a secret, but that I didn't want to have to deal with questions or any gawking.

Jasmine looked around, her brow furrowed. "Where are we?"

"Prionia, I think. I hope." I moved toward the signs that were posted in front of the log cabin serving as the starting point of the park trail. We were indeed at Prionia, thank the Gods. I would've been embarrassed if I'd taken us to a place nowhere near the mountain.

"What now?" she asked.

"From what I was able to prod out of Hephaistos—before he yelled at me to leave him alone again—we need to get to the Plateau of the Muses, and from there, we should see the door to the cyclopes stone castle in the mountain."

"Oh, so something easy." She made a face then chuckled.

"Well, at least we don't necessarily have to walk." Georgina shook her body a little, and her big white wings unfurled from her back.

"Yup, being a demigod has its bonuses." I laughed as my expansive black wings emerged as well, spreading out six feet from each shoulder. Stretching them out, I flapped them once, let them get the feel of flying again, and lifted into the air.

Jasmine and Georgina followed suit, and the three of us soared high, overtop the forest that spread out along the base of the mountain range. It felt incredible to be with my best friends again. I'd missed them more than they knew. It had been like a knife to the heart seeing them exist without me, without ever knowing me.

The thought that I would return, and they wouldn't remember me or all the amazing and loving moments we'd experienced together, was a punch to the gut. I wasn't sure I would've been able to handle that. So, I was epically relieved that it hadn't turned out that way.

We flew over the trees, and pretty waterfalls. If it had been another day, in a different circumstance, I would've liked to stroll along the meandering path through the woods, and stop on the bridge over-looking the falls to just take in its beauty. It had been a long time since I'd just done something for the fun of it. Going to Nice with Hades for the flower carnival might've been one of the last times.

Eventually, the thick forest gave way to bushes, scrub, and then rocks as the trail climbed the moun-tain. After another few minutes of flying, we reached the top, and gently lowered onto the high ridge that was named the Plateau of the Muses. I wondered if the twelve sisters had ever actually been up there. I highly doubted it. The identical looking women had always come off to me as pampered princesses, and not nature lovers.

"Okay, now that we're here," Jasmine began, "what are we looking for?"

"A door on the side of that." I gestured to the gravelly mountain looming across the valley that separated us.

We all squinted in that direction, scanning the side of the grand mass of rock protruding from the earth. I couldn't see an entrance anywhere. I did manage to spot a couple of deer gazing on the grass about halfway up the stone face.

"There!" Georgina pointed with her good arm toward the place she'd spotted. "About three feet above that large clump of bushes."

Although following her sight line, I didn't see it at first, but then something glinted in the harsh sunlight. It was something metallic. Only the tip of what had to be a huge metal door to accommodate the cyclopes could be seen affixed into the mountain.

Jasmine looked at me with a shrug. "Do we just go over there and knock?"

"Sounds like a plan to me."

We lifted into the air again, flying across the valley to the looming mountain. More of the entrance became visible the closer we got, until we were hovering in front of an iron door that was ten feet tall. Both Jasmine and Georgina looked at me expectantly. I guessed it was up to me to knock.

Getting closer, I lifted my hand to rap on the metal. The sound even reverberated outside, and I hoped it echoed enough inside that someone would answer. We waited for a few minutes, but nothing happened, so I knocked again—that time with my boot.

After waiting another couple of minutes, there was a loud clanging, some clicking, and very audible creaking as the door slowly opened to reveal a large, wide man. He stood nine feet tall, with shaggy brown hair, scruffy beard around a wide mouth, and a very large brown eye, hooded under the most impressive unibrow I'd ever seen.

The brow furrowed as he grunted. "What do you want?"

"Who is it?" Another gruff voice asked from deep inside the mountain.

"Three winged mortals," the first cyclops informed.

"Are they selling cookies?"

The cyclops's eye roamed over us, obviously looking for boxes or something. "No."

"Then tell them to go away."

Before he could tell us that, I flew closer to him
—to get in his big face. "We're not mortals. Firstly,
we are demigods, and second, we need to talk to
you about Tartarus."

He sighed, but resigned to open the door so we
could enter. We all flew in to touch down on the
stone floor. The cyclops led us further in through a
hallway, and toward what I could only call a stone
estate as grand as the castle of Versailles.

I knew that the three brothers were great crafts-
men, having taught Hephaistos everything he knew
and even creating the lightning bolt for Zeus, but
seeing what they had made firsthand was on a
whole other level.

He led us past pillars of dark stone, with intri-
cate carvings of detailed scenes on each. I ran my
fingers over the fresco, marvelling at the artistry.
Each carving was exquisite and breathtaking. I'd
thought the shadowboxes that Hephaistos had
created were beautiful, but they didn't compare to
what these three cyclopes had done.

"Your work is amazing," I finally spoke, while
we were led into a dining hall of sorts. I assumed it
was a dining hall, since the other two cyclopes were
seated at a large stone table, stuffing their faces with

what looked like some kind of large bird. Feathers were strewn everywhere. They were even stuck to their large square faces. Had they even bothered to cook it? I decided I didn't want to know.

The cyclops who had escorted us inside, grabbed what was left of the bird on the table and shoved it into his mouth. "They want to know about Tartarus, Brontes." As he chewed, he spoke, sending bits and pieces spewing out between his lips.

The larger of the two cyclops sitting at the table glared his big eye at us. I assumed he was Brontes. "Who told you to come here?"

"No one," I confessed, "but Hephaistos did tell me that if I were to come here, you would be gracious hosts."

Brontes snorted, and a feather blew out a nostril. "Hephaistos lied."

"Why do you want to know about Tartarus?" the other one at the table asked.

I considered lying, but I didn't think that would do me any good. "Because I want to know how to get inside so I can talk to Aphrodite. She has information I need."

At the mention of the Goddess, all three cyclopes tensed, and turned to glare at me. Brontes pointed a big finger in my direction. "Wait a minute, I know who you are, now. You are the Girl of Darkness. You were Hades's pet. And you killed Zeus, sending Aphrodite and Ares to prison for their treachery."

Shit. I glanced at Jasmine and Georgina, who both had yet to let down their guard—smart, a lot smarter than I, obviously—and they both shrugged. I guessed there was no point in denying the truth. I had to assume that, despite making Zeus's lightning, the brothers weren't friends with the Gods. Especially, since Aphrodite had used them to kill.

"Yes. I'm the Girl of Darkness, I guess."

Brontes slammed a ham-sized fist on the table, making everything on top of it rattle. "I'm happy that Aphrodite is in that hellish place."

I decided to take a leap of faith and hope their dislike for her would make them help us. "I know how she used you. I know what she made you do." I swallowed, waiting for their response, hoping I hadn't offended them in the process.

Brontes's eye narrowed as he growled, "How do you know?"

"Because I was there. So was she." I gestured to Jasmine. She'd been with me when we went to the

Demos' estate and found it destroyed. "I found the golden rope. My mother—"

Forced to stop, I swallowed the anger and anguish that clogged my throat. They had been compelled to cause the earthquakes that ruined much of my city, and the surrounding towns. I was trying not to look at them and put blame on their shoulders. It was hard though.

"My mother, Sophie, died in the earthquake in Pecunia."

Brontes rose to his feet, as did the other cyclops. They looked like they were going to attack us. Jasmine's hands flared to life with hot dark flames, and I could see Georgina getting ready to call to the stone itself. She could probably bring the whole thing down on our heads if she wanted.

Instead of attacking, each of them dropped to a knee and bent their heads. "We are sorry for your loss," "We cannot hope for your forgiveness, but maybe we can atone for what we've done in some way."

That, I hadn't expected, and I wasn't sure what to do about it. I had come to terms with Sophie's death years ago. Although, the pain of it still clung to my heart and flared up now and then.

Approaching Brontes, I lifted my hand over my

head. I thought about bringing down the wrath of the Gods that I held in my body upon them, but I knew that it was Aphrodite who needed to atone for what she'd done. Brontes and his brothers had been pawns in the tragedy, as much as I was.

Instead, I placed my hand on top of his head. "I forgive you." When I stepped back, a deep breath left me, hoping I would feel the forgiveness begin to heal my soul.

I didn't. I couldn't really feel much of anything right now.

With a grateful bow, the cyclops got back to his feet. "What is it that you need to know about Tartarus?"

"How to get inside. You all escaped, so I assume you know how to get back."

He nodded, gesturing to the empty chairs at the table. "Come, sit and drink. I will tell you how to go there, but I am hoping that what I say will help to change your mind. Tartarus is not a place you can ever truly leave. It stays inside you like a virus, eating away at every good thought in your mind."

CHAPTER FOURTEEN

LUCIAN

"*H*ow are we going to steal the key?" Ren asked, exasperated as we marched down the east wing corridor. "I think the girls got the long end of this stick."

I scoffed. "Ha! I don't think getting information out of three very large, very mean cyclopes is going to be anywhere near easy." Stopping, I regarded Ren. "Besides, Mel will be facing those who were responsible for the earthquakes in Pecunia. The ones who killed her mother."

Ren nodded, his face falling. "You're right. I didn't even think about that. I remember the damage in the city and the neighboring towns. It was horrific."

"So, compared to that, I think stealing a key will be a piece of cake." I slapped Ren on the back. I hadn't said what I did to make him feel badly, but I also didn't want him to discount the task that Melany chose to face. She could've asked me and Ren or anyone else to go, but she decided to do it herself, knowing full well how it would make her feel.

Though, sometimes I wondered if Melany didn't purposely put herself in painful situations. It often seemed like she was atoning for something.

We kept walking down the corridor to the weapons training room. It was part of our duty at the academy, now that we'd earned our white wings, to help train the other recruits. Ren, Melany, and I were supposed to help Artemis and Athena with sword, spear, and shield training. I wasn't sure how I was going to explain Melany's absence. Although, I was sure everyone was used to it by now.

"Do we even know what this supposed key looks like?" Ren asked as we pushed through the doors of the training center.

"My guess would be that it's big and metal."

"What if it really isn't a key, but something else altogether that opens Tartarus. What if we need to steal like a magical stone or something?"

Before I could respond, Artemis advanced on us. "You're late." Her eyes narrowed, and she looked beyond us. "And where's Melany?"

"Ah, she's not going to make it today," I informed sheepishly.

Artemis shook her head. "Eventually, that girl won't be able to use her *'wounded soldier'* pretext anymore, to get out of her duties at the academy. We all lost friends and people we care about in the battle. It is part of being a warrior and a demigod."

She didn't stay to hear my excuses, marching back to stand in front of the group of new recruits. Ren and I joined her, and I immediately spotted Cassandra within the group. Once again, she stood in the back, away from the others.

When her head came up and our gazes met, something surprising zipped through me. I wasn't certain what it was—a familiarity of sorts, more than just being an acquaintance—but it made me uncomfortable. She must've felt it as well, because she immediately dropped her gaze, her cheeks flushing pink.

Artemis and Athena put the recruits through

their paces, as well as pushing me and Ren hard until we were both sweating. Once I finished sparring with a few of the more experienced recruits, I had to spar with Cassandra.

I gave her one of the blunted swords that we used to train—no one wanted to run anyone through quite yet. Putting my hands over hers, I showed her how to hold it. Her cheeks blushed again while I stood behind her, helping her take up the proper stance. The smell of her hair, lilacs and vanilla, was like a punch in the gut. Again, it was so familiar.

Shifting around to stand in front of her, I took my fighting stance. "Now swing your sword at me."

She hesitated, biting on her lower lip.

"Don't worry, you won't hurt me."

Nodding, Cassandra gripped the hilt tightly with both hands and swung, aiming for my shoulder. I blocked it and took a step back. She swung again, this time down toward my leg—a good volley. Once more, I blocked and stepped back. Then, as if possessed by Athena herself, Cassandra spun and brought her blade around. It was a perfect attack, and the blunted blade struck me across the side. If we'd been using real steel, that would've been a fatal blow.

My eyebrows rose, and I tipped my head. "Well done. You're a natural."

At that, a bright smile curved her lips, and I was punched in the gut yet again. It was almost staggering. What was going on? I shouldn't have been feeling that way about her. It didn't make sense.

We continued to spar, back and forth, and so evenly matched that we gained a bit of an audience. Artemis and Athena both stopped to watch. After exchanging volleys and hits, I was surprised at the stamina Casandra showed. She'd seemed so timid before, that I, along with everyone else, had misjudged her strength and skills. Apollo said she was an extraordinary prophet, but I thought she was a skilled swordsman as well.

After she aimed at my shoulder again, I dodged it, swung around and swiped at her leg. My blade hit her hard in the calf, making her trip, and she fell onto her side. The crowd that had gathered around us started to clap.

"Well done, Cassandra," Athena praised. "You will be a fearsome fighter in battle."

Smiling, I offered my hand to help Cassandra stand, and as soon as she took it, I yanked her up. I must've pulled her too hard, because she ran right into me. Instead of backing off, though, she wrapped an arm around my neck and pulled my head down to her mouth.

"I know where the key is."

Surprised, I eyed her. "Did you see it in one of your visions?"

"No, when I was in his office. Apollo took me to see Prometheus after I healed in the infirmary."

"Are you sure it was the key to Tartarus?"

She nodded. "I'm positive." Letting go of me, she took a few steps back.

Disappointment flooded through me when she let me go, surprising me.

Others had noticed though, including Ren, who was giving me a "What the hell?" look from across the room.

I ignored him and went back to training with the other recruits.

Later, in the dining hall, Ren ambushed me. "What was that? Are you digging Cassandra now?"

"It wasn't like that." I filled my plate with as much as I could carry—I'd worked up a mighty appetite. "She told me she knows where the key is."

"Okay, so did she also tell you how we're going to get it?"

We sat down at our usual table. "No, but it's in Prometheus's office."

"And how are we going to get into his office when he's in there."

"We need to find a time when he's not there, I guess."

I took a few bites of the hamburger and some fries while the gears ground in my mind. Then I heard Dionysus chatting up a couple of the Muse sisters in the corner of the dining room—maybe Clio and Thalia, it was near impossible to tell them apart—and I came up with a plan. Getting up, I went over to talk to him.

He nodded to me when I approached. "Hey, Lucian. What's up? Where's that girl of yours?" He looked around the dining hall. "I'm sure she owes me a favor or two, and I'd like to collect."

"Ah, she's running some errands for Hephaistos."

Dionysus looked at me dubiously. "You're not a very good liar." He chuckled. "I could give you a few lessons on that, if you like?"

"I'll think about it, but what I was wondering was when you were going to throw another gig. I've told a few of the new recruits about the music you spin, and they can't wait to hear it. Told them they'd never hear anyone as good as you are at spinning."

"Ain't that the truth. I am definitely the best. I taught Daft Punk everything they know. Did I tell you that before?"

"Nope, but I'd love to hear about it. How about tonight? We haven't had a big blowout in months. I'm pretty sure everyone could use some fun."

His hand smacked my the shoulder. "I like your style, Lucian."

"You should do it up huge. Invite everyone. In fact, the other day, Prometheus told me he'd love to hear your music."

"Really?" He gave me a look.

"Yup. It would be an honor."

He rubbed at the smudged black eye makeup on his cheek. "All right. Let's do it." A wide grin stretched his mouth as he looked to the two Muses. "You're coming right?"

They both nodded.

"And you'll bring your ten other sisters, hey?"

After planting the seed, I left him to plan, hoping that Prometheus would take the bait.

That night, true to form, Dionysus pulled out all the stops and put on an epic party in the Great Hall. The golden room was decked out with silly balloons and streamers, much like a junior high dance in the gymnasium of a school. That paired with decadent pastries and designer cocktails, smoke machines, lasers, and bubbles. The music he spun thumped hard, vibrating the floor underneath our feet.

I took it all in, remembering the first party we all attended when we first got to the academy. The memory of dancing with Melany and how caustic and snide she'd been about it played in my mind. I smiled; she honestly hadn't softened all that much, just in the important ways.

Ren nudged me with his elbow. "What do we do if Prometheus doesn't show?"

"I don't know. Tell him the truth and ask him for the key?" I replied sarcastically.

Ren shook his head. "Yeah, pretty sure that wouldn't work."

Yeah, the truth wasn't something the Gods dabbled in much. It was usually lies, secrets, and betrayal. To be fair, some things had changed since Prometheus took over the running of the academy, but there were still many of the old Gods left who I sensed weren't that happy about Zeus's demise.

Demeter, looking completely out of place in her flowered sundress, suede tasselled vest and bare feet —there were even flowers in her long wavy hair—

approached us as we hovered near the drinks and food table. I had a drink in my hand but had yet to take a sip of it.

Her gaze swept over me, Ren, and Cassandra, then around the room. "Where's the rest of you?"

"Ah, not sure."

She smirked. "Right. Why do I get the sense that you're up to something? Again."

"I don't know what you mean."

She leaned in closer to me. "Just be careful. Heph told me about the shadowboxes and the things Melany told him. Time and Fate is not something you want to mess around with." Then she wandered away.

Ren glanced at me, obviously wanting to know what she'd said, but I didn't get a chance before Cassandra nudged me and gestured toward the door. Prometheus had just arrived.

"Okay, Ren, you're the distraction. You keep him talking and here in this room, while Cassandra and I go to his office."

He nodded, and moved through the crowd toward Prometheus. Swiftly, Cassandra and I made our way out the main doors. Once in the corridor, we walked a bit faster, but not enough to rouse suspicion. The last thing we needed was to be detained by one of the guards situated around the academy, or by any of the Gods.

Prometheus's office was in Zeus's Hall. Made sense, as the lightning God wasn't using it anymore. That was good. As a member of Zeus's clan, I had access to the hall since my room was there. So, the guards wouldn't stop me from entering.

As we neared the entrance to the hall, which was in the highest tower in the academy, I grabbed Cassandra's hand. She gave me a look.

"Just in case they ask," I offered, motioning toward the guards.

Realization of what I'd suggested dawned in her eyes, and she blushed again.

I nodded to them, Bishop and Harmon were their names, as we walked past. They nodded in return but didn't stop us. Once in the hall, and out of sight from anyone, I pointed upward to the highest point in the tower. "We need to go up there. You'll need to grab onto me, so I can fly us up. It'll take too long to take the stairs."

Cassandra wrapped her arms around my shoulders, and I put my arms around her waist, then unfurled my wings and lifted us. As I flew up the six stories, I was acutely aware of how she felt in my arms. It made me feel very uncomfortable, not because it was awkward, but because it felt intimate, like we'd done it a million times before.

Something had changed when Melany returned from Asphodel Meadows. She'd told us about a timeline where she didn't exist. A reality where Zeus still lived, the big battle hadn't happened, we still had our powers, and where Melany and I hadn't been together. None of us could remember such a reality, thank the Gods, but I had a sense that maybe Cassandra still did.

Melany and she had shared some kind of understanding about it all. Yet, I was afraid to ask about it, because deep down I knew what it meant. Scent and touch were two senses that carried powerful memories, and mine were telling me the truth.

Once at the top, I released Cassandra, and moved away from her. Probably too quickly, judging by the hurt look on her face, but that wasn't something I was willing to deal with right now. We had other important things to take care of first.

"Where did you see the key?"

"Over there." She pointed toward the right side of the bookcase that wrapped around the circular room.

We rushed over to the shelves she indicated.

There were books stacked everywhere, but there were also a few old trinkets displayed—like an old looking glass that sailors would've used. Next to it was a compass, also old, and beside it sat a decorative wooden box. Frowning, Cassandra pushed the box around, and the compass.

"It was right here."

"Maybe he moved it." I began searching the other shelves. "What does it look like?"

"Like an old, metal skeleton key. It's large, black iron, has some weird symbols carved into it."

We searched through all the shelves in the room but didn't find it. "He must have it on him," I concluded.

"Maybe, then how do we get it?"

Frustrated, I shrugged. "I don't know, but let's get out of here before we are caught."

I flew us down from the platform, and we left the hall. Thankfully, neither Bishop nor Harmon said anything as we walked out the large golden doors. Defeat flooded me as we moved through the corridors and back to the Great Hall. I didn't want to disappoint Melany, especially after all that she'd been through recently.

As we strode, I glanced over at Cassandra. She was quiet, which was usual, but the look on her face told me that she was feeling more than just disappointment at not having found the key.

"Hey, I don't know exactly what's going on—although I kind of have a notion. I feel like I should apologize to you..."

She shook her head. "Please don't. It's hard enough as it is. I don't want or need your pity."

Reaching for her arm, I stopped her from walking. "It's not pity, Cassandra. It never would be. Ever. It's just..."

"I get it, Lucian. In this life, in this time, Melany is alive and well. I could never hope to compete with that. With her." She pulled out of my grasp and continued walking.

I let her go ahead of me.

When we returned to the Great Hall, the party was in full swing. I spotted Ren in the corner, talking to Prometheus, who looked utterly bored. Ren caught my gaze with a lift of his eyebrows. I shook my head, and his face dropped.

Prometheus took that moment of distraction to slip away, and Ren let him go, then rushed across the room to talk to me.

"What happened?"

"We couldn't find it. It wasn't where Cassandra saw it. It has to be on him."

"Damn it."

I was about to agree with him, when something caught my eye near the main doors. The shadows opened up and Melany, Jasmine, and Georgina literally stumbled out of them. Georgina nearly fell onto her face, but the other two grabbed her arms before she could.

The three of us rushed over to them to find out what had happened. The moment I got close I could smell alcohol. It was wafting off all three of them like waves of perfume. I inspected their faces, realizing they were drunk. Or at the very least, on their way to being drunk.

"What happened to you?"

Melany waved a hand around like she was conducting an orchestra. "The cyclopes like to drink."

"And so do the three of you, obviously." Ren chuckled.

"They had a long story to tell us, and kept filling our cups full of ale to tell it." Melany's voice slurred a little.

"Did you get the information at least."

She nodded but Georgina stumbled forward. "Damn rights we got it! Because we are fearless warriors!" Georgina blurted.

Out of the three of them, she was in the worst condition. She could barely stand, having to be held up by Melany and Jasmine.

"Did you get the key?" Melany asked.

"No. It wasn't in his office, so we figure he has it on him."

Before she could curse up a storm, the afore-mentioned Prometheus walked right toward us. When he spotted Ren, he sort of changed direc-tions, so he could easily bypass us without having to stop to talk. I had a sense Ren had talked his ear off.

As he neared, I caught a glimpse of his belt under his lengthy robes. It had several metal things hanging from it, including the key we needed. Cassandra had been right, it was large and black. And when I squinted just right, the symbols etched along the body of it glinted faintly. There was no mistaking it.

Georgina mumbled something under her breath, and we all looked at her quizzically.

"Let me go," she whispered.

At first, Melany glanced at Jasmine with a frown, but then, I think they both understood what she wanted. They released their hold on her arms, and she went stumbling forward, running right into

Prometheus. Instinctively, he grabbed a hold of her before she could fall.

"Whoa, there." He chuckled. "I think maybe you've had too much to drink."

I went to take her from him. "Sorry about that, sir. I'll make sure she gets back to her hall safely."

He nodded to me, looked over at the others, then basically pushed Georgina over to me, before walking away down the corridor. I swore he mumbled, "Gods, why did I take this job," before disappearing around the corner.

When he was gone, Georgina fell onto the ground, rolling over onto her back. Grinning, she held up her hand. Inside it was the key. She started to laugh manically. "I'm a Gods damn warrior!"

We all laughed with her. It felt good to have a laugh, as I suspected we weren't going to get another chance for some time.

CHAPTER FIFTEEN

MELANY

The next morning, under the cover of pre-dawn, Lucian, Jasmine, Georgina— who was suffering from a major hangover—Ren, Cassandra, and I assembled on the bank of the lake, again. I'd given everyone the choice to accompany me or not, although I would've preferred to go alone, because I didn't want anyone to get hurt. I also knew that I didn't want to make that decision for anyone. They knew the risks.

Besides that, I figured we'd need everyone's varying degree of skills and powers to safely get to

Tartarus. It was going to be an arduous journey based on the information we got from the cyclopes.

The only one's presence I questioned was Cassandra's. Her visions had certainly helped us thus far, and I did consider her part of the crew, it was just that she didn't seem to have any other skill that would be useful and she didn't have wings, so one of us was going to have to carry her.

I said as much at the lake's edge, but Lucian defended her. "She's got skill with a sword. I'd go as far as saying she's just about as good as you, Mel."

When I regarded Cassandra, she shrunk against my look. She had a sword in a scabbard affixed to her belt, and wore it like she knew what to do with it, so I wasn't about to test that theory. I'd take Lucian at his word.

"Okay." I didn't ask who was going to carry her when we had to fly, because I assumed Lucian had already decided to take on that roll. The image of them together popped up in my head, and I wondered if I was subconsciously pushing them together, as a way to alleviate my guilt at mourning so long for Hades. Maybe. Right now, it didn't matter, so I pushed it out of my mind.

"So," Ren broke the ice, looking around, "what are we doing here?"

I made sure everyone had brought weapons, since from what Brontes told us about Tartarus we would definitely going to need them. I also had a couple of backpacks filled with rope, pegs, chisel, water and food. Because Brontes also mentioned a lot of rocks, cliffs, and deep chasms. We were probably going to have to be a bunch of spelunkers. Although we were winged, I wasn't sure how dependable the air was going to be to fly.

"Our first step is to get down to the underworld," I began, "and although my shadow walking seems to have fixed itself for the most part, I am still blocked from getting into Hades's Hall. So, we're going to go old school, and use Hecate's oak tree to get down to the tunnels that lead to the underworld."

Ren nodded; he'd been with Lucian and the others when they came looking for me after Hades kidnapped me, and took me to his hall.

I led everyone into the woods and to the tree stump that was once Hecate's massive oak tree and home. It was still cracked open from when I'd used it to get travel down a couple of weeks ago. For a moment, as we walked, I thought maybe we wouldn't find the stump. That it had disappeared or something after the two timelines had merged, but thankfully it was still there. The cut trunk sat open enough that we could drop, one by one, into the tunnel that would lead us to the open, barren field, and eventually get us to the river Styx.

Then the journey would get hard.

We crossed the barren plains without any problems. When we reached the river's edge, I had déjà vu, and wondered if Cerberus was going to emerge from the rushing black water to greet me. I secretly wished that to come true, but it wasn't the three-headed hellhound I needed to see for this part of our odyssey.

"Charon!" I shouted over the churning river toward the cave that led to Hades's Hall. "Charon! I need your help!"

I wasn't sure if the skeletal butler would show up, but I remembered Hades told me once that Charon would see to my every need, no matter what need that was. Well, I needed to sail down the River Styx to find the entrance to Tartarus.

"What if he doesn't show?" Lucian asked. "Can we swim the river ourselves?"

Honestly, I didn't know the answer to that question, but what I did know was that no one had ever gone into the River Styx without a boat and come out again. Even Poseidon couldn't swim the cursed water. Hades had designed it that way, so his brothers couldn't ever attack him and survive.

"Charon! Please, I need your help!" calledWhat I didn't say out loud was that he'd told me that I would rule the underworld one day. Hades had left it for me, so he better obey me now.

A thick fog rolled out from the cave's entrance and hovered near the river on the opposite shore from where we stood. Out from the mist, a cloaked figure emerged, and I smiled. It was Charon. He'd heard my silent request.

"It's good to see you again, my lady." Charon inclined his skeletal head toward me.

The others all gaped. I hadn't told any of them about what Charon had confessed, and how he regarded me.

"I need a favor, Charon," I shouted across the bend.

"All you have to do is ask."

"We need transport down the river."

Charon lifted a bony arm toward the water, and it started to boil and foam. Everyone took a step back when a boat, well much more than a boat, a ship really, emerged from beneath the surface. A wooden plank smacked down on the river's edge, inviting us aboard.

"Holy shit," Jasmine murmured.

To make sure it was safe, I crossed the plank first and stepped onto the boat. I turned and beckoned the others to come on board. One by one they crossed the wooden platform and settled with me, each taking a seat on one of the benches in the middle. Once we were all aboard, the plank magically disappeared.

Charon floated across the water, and stepped up on to the bow of the vessel to steer us in the right direction with his long wooden pole. "Now, shall we go?" he asked.

Positioning myself at the front, I nodded to him, and the boat settled into the water, taking us down the river at a swift pace.

Lucian came to stand beside me. "I thought the river only went in a giant circle around the underworld."

"It does, but Brontes said we should see a swirling mass of dark clouds along the way. When we do, we have to get off the boat as quick as possible before the funnel disappears. The funnel will point us to the gate."

As we swept down the river, the front of the boat bumped into rocks periodically, sending us swaying to the side. I looked down into the dark water. Once in a while I thought I saw something floating. At first, I thought it was the waving leaves of plant matter reaching up to the surface, in search of a sunlight that would never come, but after seeing it a few more times, my stomach roiled over with realization.

"What's in the water, Charon?" The waver in my voice drew the attention of the others, and they all peered into the river with a wariness I wish I'd respected.

"The River Styx holds the souls of those who are trying to cross over from life to death. Some are stuck here for an eternity."

Swallowing down the bile rising in my throat, I looked over the boat's edge, and unfortunately, saw things more clearly. Now, instead of the waving sprouts of weeds, I saw the reaching, grasping arms and hands of damned souls. Hundreds of them.

"Oh, Gods. That's horrible." Georgina pulled away from the side and hugged herself.

Reaching over for her, Jasmine grabbed her hand. "Don't look."

I tore my gaze away from the souls and focused on the barren land surrounding us. "Everyone, be on the lookout for a funnel of clouds. The second we spot it, we have to get off this boat if we want to find the entrance to Tartarus."

Everyone drew back from the edges, and looked over to the desolate land we were sailing past.

Since time moved differently in the underworld, I wasn't sure how long it was. In some ways, it felt like hours had passed, and others, it felt like mere minutes. Cassandra stood up from the bench and pointed toward something in the distance, on the shore.

"There. I saw a swirling of dark clouds."

Looking toward the spot she'd pointed toward, I didn't see anything at first, but then I got a glimpse of a funnel of shadows swirling around like a narrow tornado.

"Charon! We need to get off the boat!"

True to his word, he stopped the boat by jamming his pole into the bottom of the river. Everyone jerked forward from the sudden stop, and both Jasmine and Cassandra fell of the benches, landing on their knees onto the wooden hull.

A plank suddenly slammed onto the shore of the river, and we all got off the boat. I turned to thank Charon, but just as he'd suddenly appeared out of the thick fog, he disappeared and the ship with him. We were on our own.

"C'mon! We need to get to it before it disappears!" My wings unfurled, but I already knew the air here was different, denser, and it wouldn't be so easy to just fly there. It would still be faster than running.

The others opened their wings and took to the sky, though it proved hard for everyone to get airborne and fly easily. It was even harder for Lucian because he had to carry Cassandra with him, but eventually we were all in the air, soaring toward the swirling mass of clouds.

It was difficult to pinpoint the tornado's true location because it kept moving. It would swirl down, making contact with the ground, zip back up into the clouds, and then spin around somewhere else. We got closer to it—the roaring sound of its wind echoed all around us.

Lifting my hand, I signaled for everyone to stop, so we all hovered in the sky, with the dark clouds spinning in front of us. Brontes explained we had to wait until the funnel touched the ground and stayed there, and it would reveal the gate.

Another funnel formed, inching out of the cloud like a tentacle. It reached for the ground, touched, lifted, and touched again, seemingly starting to dig into the earth like a drill bit.

Excited, I pointed. "There!" I dove toward the area where the tornado was spinning around making a dirt storm.

The closer I got, the stronger the winds became. Dirt and grit peppered my face, getting into my eyes, but I pushed on, flying closer. In the end it became too hard to stay in the air, and I touched down, folded up my wings and walked, pushing against the strong winds, toward the hole the funnel was making.

After glancing over my shoulder to make sure the others had also landed, they had, I continued until I was a just a few feet away from the eye of the storm. The wind was strong there, tearing at my clothes and hair, but there was no turning back now.

Lucian came up along one side with Cassandra and Ren, while Jasmine and Georgina came up on the other side. I reached over and grabbed Lucian's hand then Jasmine's. To get through the funnel we were going to need to do it together.

I nodded to them both. We all stepped forward. Leaning into the winds, we walked through the swirling clouds, and came out on the other side— the middle, where everything was calm and quiet. The difference was disconcerting. Once we were through, we looked at the ground and saw what the tornado had uncovered.

It was indeed a gate. A large, iron gate with a lock. When I glanced over at Cassandra, she held out the key that had been hanging around her neck. I took it from her, then walked onto the lattice of thick metal bars and slid the key into the padlock, turning it slowly. The clanking of the tumblers echoed in the eerie silence, disengaging.

With a final click, the gate swung open, and I plunged into a one hundred-foot abyss.

CHAPTER SIXTEEN

MELANY

*M*y stomach roiled as I dropped.

It was so sudden, I couldn't get my wings to expand. I reached out toward the side of the hole, to find something to grab onto, but dirt crumbled in my hands.

Yet, before I could plummet to my death, Georgina snatched me by the wrist with her metal hand, and I came to an abrupt halt, with a rip of pain. I was pretty sure my shoulder had popped out of its joint.

"I got you," she said between gritted teeth.

My neck craned up, to see that she did have me,

and Lucian, Jasmine, Ren, and even Cassandra had her. It was like a daisy chain of friends saving my ass.

Slowly, she pulled me up, every inch sending a jolt of pain through my body. When she finally got me out of the hole, I rolled over onto my back on the ground, holding my arm. "My shoulder got jacked. I'm going to need for someone to push it back in."

Georgina crouched next to me. "Sit up."

I did, and holding my wrist, she set her metal hand against my elbow, moving it inwards. I hissed through the pain, until I heard a pop, and she pushed my joint right back into where it should've been. When she was done, she let me go.

"How does that feel?"

Slowly, I rotated it. There was still a bit of an ache, but the shoulder was definitely relocated. "It's okay."

Placing a hand onto my skin, she sent her healing power into me until a lovely, warm glow soothed me, traveling all the way down my arm. I grinned, as it almost made me feel giddy.

"Thanks, Gina."

After Lucian helped me back to my feet, we all

gathered on the edge of the chasm, peeking into it. It was so deep that no light hit the bottom.

"Did good old Brontes warn you about this?" Lucian asked.

I shook my head. "Nope, he just said it would be a hole."

Putting her hands together, Jasmine created a ball of fire between them, about the size of a grape-fruit. She dropped it into the hole. We watched it go down, and down, and down, revealing rings of dirt then jagged rock along the sides, until it was barely a pinpoint of light where it seemed to land. Then, it blinked out of existence.

"Gods, that's a long way down." Ren moved back, wiping away the sweat that had beaded on his brow.

"Good thing we have wings," I mumbled.

"Doesn't look wide enough for them," Jasmine warned.

"If the hole can fit the expanse of a cyclops, it will accommodate our wings."

Stepping closer, to what I thought was the center of the width of the hole I unfurled mine to measure it. From tip to tip, it appeared to be enough room, but of course, from up here we couldn't determine if the chasm was as wide up

here as it was down there. For all we knew, it could
narrow into a space big enough for the grapefruit-
sized fire ball and nothing else. The only way we
were going to find out was by going down there.

It was our only option anyway.

"We could use the rope, as a precaution,"
Lucian suggested.

"You could lower me down to test the width of
the hole." Cassandra already had the rope out of
the backpack she'd been carrying.

I could tell Lucian wanted to protest, but I also
knew Cassandra wanted to feel like she was
contributing to the mission, and she wasn't a
burden. I reached for the rope. "Can you carry a
fireball with you, so we can see your progress?"

She nodded.

Ten minutes later, the rope was tied around
Cassandra's waist, and as a group, we were lowering
her into the chasm. Jasmine had formed another
ball of fire for her, setting it in her hands. Cassandra
had already been through fire training with
Hephaistos, and knew how to handle the flames so
they wouldn't burn her.

Two things became evident fairly quickly—the
chasm wasn't as narrow as we'd feared, and
Cassandra was a lot tougher than anyone gave her

credit for, well, that I gave her credit for. I had a feeling the others, in particular, Lucian, thought she was bad ass.

After determining that we could fly down, we pulled Cassandra back up and prepared to make the descent. Using the rope again, I helped Lucian tie Cassandra to him, so he would be free to use his hands.

I decided I would go down first. Unfolding my wings, I tested them with a few good flaps, and stepped out into thin air, hovering there for moment. Slowly, I began to make my way down, igniting fire in my hands as I descended. Soon, layers of dirt gave way to rock, the further down I went, the more jagged they became.

Another thing I noticed was the air temperature. Up top, it was stagnant, neither hot nor cold, just tepid, but deep in the hole it was starting to get cold. Brontes did warn me about it. He described Tartarus as a bitterly barren and desolate landscape of craggy rock, with ice crystals sharp enough to skewer a person.

I supposed, I hadn't expect the type of cold we would encounter. It seemed to penetrate skin and flesh instantly. By the time I reached the bottom I was shivering, my breath coming out in plumes. Not just because of the brittleness in the air, but because of what I saw emerging from beyond the hole in the earth.

It was Tartarus, and it was terrifying.

Waiting for the others to reach me, I hovered there, looking across the great expanse of bleak wasteland that was the ultimate prison. It was a huge cave of sorts, with craggy rock above, and craggy rock below. It wasn't fully dark; it had a light source somewhere in the vast distance. Whatever it was, didn't produce warmth-giving sunlight, but just a white luminance that bathed the entire landscape in a colorless obscurity. And I'd thought Asphodel Meadows had been dreary and dismal. There was no comparison. The meadows had been pure joy compared to this.

When the others dropped out of the hole and hovered beside me, I saw the same stunned looks on their faces that I had.

"Good Gods," Lucian murmured.

"Yeah, I don't know about that," I mumbled.

"This place is big," Ren noted. "Where are we going to find Aphrodite and Ares?"

"Well, everyone needs a place to sleep, whether you're a God or not. So, let's scout out anything that looks like it could be used for shelter." I reached over my shoulder to make sure my bow and quiver of arrows were still affixed to my back. I had no doubt in my mind that I was going to have a use for them down there.

As a unit, we soared over the stretch of land, looking for anything—a hut, a house, a castle—that could serve as shelter. For the most part, we found just rocky cliffs and jagged points of stone that seemed like large spearheads, sticking out of the ground. Nothing appeared remotely inhabitable.

Eventually, I spotted a source of water, a pond of some sort, that had moss and low-lying scrub around its shore. I pointed it out and suggested we land nearby. Water meant life. If anyone was going to set up camp anywhere in this place, it would be next to a source of water. That would just be the most logical action.

Once on the ground, I got a full realization of this place. It was not a place I would wish on many people. Although, it did give me a little bit of satisfaction to know that the Goddess of Love and Light, the most treacherous bitch I'd ever come across, was imprisoned here. I wondered how she faired without all of her luxuries.

We didn't have to wait long for that answer.

A barrage of rocks rained down on us from

somewhere above on one of the cliffs. Luckily, they weren't huge, or one or more of us would've been beaned in the head and dropped. As it was, they hit a few of us in the shoulders and arms—there would be bruises for sure—before Georgina constructed a wall of stone, like a shield, to protect us.

Peering around the barrier, I found Ares leaping off the cliff and landing nearby—a homemade spear in one hand, and a wooden shield in the other. He looked like a madman, with long scraggily hair and beard, torn toga, fur vest, and bare feet. His wings were dingy, and some of the feathers appeared clipped.

With a war cry, he charged toward us.

I nocked an arrow and fired at him. He blocked it with this shield, the arrow tip imbedding into it, but kept coming. I wouldn't get another arrow knocked before his spear pierced my chest. Leaping out of our stone barrier, Lucian unsheathed his sword and blocked Ares' advance, but the god hadn't lost his ability while imprisoned. In fact, he seemed fiercer, almost animal like in his attack.

Armed with his knives, Ren stepped out, but he wasn't a match to Ares' deft handle of the spear. Ren had to do a lot of ducking and dodging to avoid that sharp tip. Jasmine joined him with her sword. She charged at Ares, but he hindered her strike, pushing her back with his shield. She landed on her back, almost falling into the pond.

"I just want to talk." The wild look his in eyes told me he was beyond any form of communication. "Aphrodite!" I shouted into the air, knowing full well she was nearby, probably watching the whole thing with glee. "I just want to talk to you. I need some information."

The sound of huge flapping wings echoed from above, and I turned just as a giant eagle swept down from the cliffs. Its claws pinched my shoulders, effectively blocking my wings from unfurling before I could react, and she lifted me into the air. I considered setting her claws and feet on fire, but it was a short way down, and I wasn't sure I could get my wings out before I hit the jagged rocks below us.

Eventually, she dropped me on the cliff, settling herself on top of my body. Her claws still pierced my flesh while the weight of her body crushed my chest. Aphrodite was heavy as a giant eagle. She lowered her sharp beak toward my throat.

"I only came here to talk to you. I don't want to kill you, but I will." My hands lit up with flames and I lifted them toward her feathery body.

She must've figured I would do it, because she

stepped off me, standing on her eagle legs, and folded her big wings into her body—starting to shift back. After a few minutes, Aphrodite stood before me.

Her once long golden hair was now choppy, as if cut with a dull blade, lank and dark from being unwashed. Her face and arms were streaked with dirt. Her dress was torn, and her bare feet looked cut up and bruised from walking around on the rocks for months. For a moment, I almost felt sorry for her, but then I remembered everything she'd done to my friends and me, and every ounce of pity bled out of my body.

She was instrumental in Sophie's death… and in Hades's. I would never, could never forgive her.

CHAPTER SEVENTEEN

MELANY

"What do you want?" Aphrodite croaked, her voice no longer like milk and honey.

"Call off your dog," I demanded,

"Now, why would I do that?"

"Because we have food. Real food. Fruit, and I think some pastries too."

Her eyes lit up, and I could imagine what they'd been feasting on down here. If it was anything like what Hecate had resorted to eating in Asphodel Meadows... my stomach roiled with the memory.

"We could just kill you and take it anyway." She took a threatening step toward me.

As a Goddess, she was strong and could shapeshift into pretty much anything, but I'd never seen her in a real fight. Aphrodite hadn't done much in the Battle of Pecunia, except stand there, watching and gloating. She didn't have a weapon on her as far as I could see, yet I knew she was still dangerous.

"There are six of us and two of you. We all have powers and weapons. How long do you really think you'll last?" To make my point I held out my hands, and narrow ribbons of lightning curled around my fingers. I could send a bolt toward her in seconds, and she knew it. She had seen me destroy Zeus, I imagined she was calculating her odds of surviving me.

"Ares! Don't kill them!" she shouted.

Moving toward the edge of the cliff, I looked down at the others. Immediately, Ares lowered his spear and retreated, but Lucian swung his sword around, looking to attack.

"Lucian, don't kill him!"

He glanced up at me, nodding, but didn't sheath his sword.

"Give me this food now," she snarled.

"Okay." I spread my wings, my shoulders aching again from the gouges her eagle claws had made, and I flew down to the pond.

As she followed me, I noticed her wings were missing a few feathers, like Ares's. I wondered what creatures they'd tangled with to damage them that way.

I took the backpack that Georgina had been carrying and tossed it to Aphrodite. She tore it open, grasped the apple inside with her bony hand and took a big bite out of it, core and all. Bits of it came out as she chewed. Seeing what she was eating, Ares rushed toward her and pulled the backpack away—nearly knocking her over. His hand reached in to grab whatever he could, and he shoved a pear into his mouth.

My vile rose as I watched them eat. They had only been in Tartarus for six months, but I could just imagine what they'd be like in a few years, in a few decades. In a millennia, as the Titans had been imprisoned.

"Now you can answer my questions," I reminded.

"What do you want to know?" she spat, as she chewed the Danish Ren had insisted on packing.

"I want to know where the Cave of Memory is, and how to get there."

Halting her eating, she gave me a perplexed look. "Why do you want to go there?"

As if she didn't know. I smirked. "To stop you from resurrecting Zeus."

Aphrodite barked out a laugh. "What are you on about? I think all that power swirling around in you has finally driven you stupid."

"You've been messing around with the Fates and with time."

Her expression contorted as she regarded me. "Uh huh, and how do you think I've been doing that? I'm in hell, if you haven't noticed. Thanks to you."

Taken a back, I glanced over at the others, they were all looking at me with confusion. Had I been wrong? It wasn't Aphrodite playing around with time and death? If not her, then who?

"Thanatos told me you've been to see the Fates. Is that true?"

She licked the sticky icing off her fingers. "I may have gone to see them, over two thousand years ago."

"So, you know where they are and how to get there. I need you to tell me."

"And what will you do for me?"

Shrugging, I gestured to the backpack. "You already ate it. Maybe you should've thought about saving some of it for later, considering you're going to be here for an eternity."

"Nothing lasts for an eternity, little girl. You must know that by now." She smirked. "Hades knew that all too well."

I didn't like the snide way she talked about him. I slid out an arrow and knocked it on my bow. I aimed it at her. "Watch your tongue, or this arrow will fly right into your mouth and come out of the other side with your tongue stuck on the tip."

"Then you won't have your information. Information I realize now is very important to you. And is worth something for us."

Shit. I hadn't counted on her asking for favors. I should've remembered how manipulative and devious she was. That was a big mistake.

"We're not going to help you escape this place, if that's what you're asking." Although, I supposed they could escape all on their own. We did leave the gate unlocked and open in our haste to get down here, but she didn't know that.

Before Aphrodite could respond, a thundering roar resounded all around us, bouncing off the craggy rock. Instinctively, I moved towards Lucian and the others just as a large blue shape in the sky flew toward us.

"It's Khione," Aphrodite grumbled.

"Who is Khione?" I asked.

"She is the Goddess of Winter and Ice, and not someone I've seen in thousands of years." She pointed an accusatory finger at me. "You brought her here as revenge against me."

"I didn't. I didn't even know she existed. I didn't know a Goddess could be a creature."

"She wasn't always one."

It was at that point that I realized the reason for Aphrodite's fear—which I could feel wafting of her in waves—was that she'd turned Khione into that.

"Someone sent her after me. Who knew you were coming here?"

Pausing, I went over everyone I'd talked to about this in my mind. Thanatos would assume I'd come, so would Hecate, but that was it. Not even Hephaistos knew what I'd been truly up to, because I hadn't even had a chance to tell him about Asphodel Meadows.

"Nobody."

She barked out a humorless laugh. "You are still such a foolish girl. Secrets can't be kept at the academy. Someone always knows. Someone is always watching, especially when it comes to you."

I didn't know what that last bit meant, but I didn't have time to mull it over before the big blue dragon with pale blue eyes swooped over us, breathing a stream of ice like a laser. Her ice breath hit the pond, freezing the water instantly.

We all jumped into battle mode, so I drew out an arrow from my quiver and knocked it. "Jasmine! Light me up!"

Flames igniting on her fingers, she ran over to me, and set them to the tip of my arrow. It took a moment but it caught on fire. Aiming into the sky, I waited until the dragon came around again, letting my arrow loose.

It whizzed by her big scaley head. The arrow didn't hit her, but it was enough to get her attention, and as she roared again, her piercing gaze narrowed in on me. I wasn't sure if that was what I wanted. All I knew was that I had to keep Aphrodite alive, so she could give me the information I desperately needed.

Knocking another arrow, I had Jasmine light it up, and let it loose. That time I aimed for the dragon's wing, I didn't want to kill her as I didn't have a quarrel with her, but I couldn't let the dragon kill

Aphrodite either. It was a very strange conundrum to be in, considering I'd wished death on Aphrodite a thousand times.

"We need to incapacitate the dragon," I called to the others. "And we have to protect Aphrodite."

Lucian's eyebrows hit his hairline. "That's not something I ever thought I'd hear you say."

"Me either, but here we are."

"Okay, what do you want us to do?"

"Distract it, maybe?"

He nodded, then flapped his wings and took to the air. Ren, Georgina, and Jasmine followed him up, leaving Cassandra on the ground looking a bit like a frightened child, but she withdrew her sword and took a stance next to me.

A couple of fire balls formed on Jasmine's hands while the dragon came around again, breathing another penetrating laser of ice that cut through the stone of the cliff nearby. Boulders fell down, one of them nearly hitting Georgina, but she was able to swerve out of the way.

I grabbed Aphrodite's arm tightly and shook her. "Tell me what you know."

"Why would I do that? You'll let Khione kill me once I do."

No, I wouldn't let that happen, would I? Maybe. Probably.

"I won't, although you definitely deserve it. How many lives have you ruined?"

"Countless." She gave me a defiant look, but there was something in her eyes that told me maybe she was getting weary of being the villain.

Ares decided to take that moment to defend his lover against me, although I wasn't an immediate threat to her. Grabbing me from behind, he put a carved down piece of stone to my throat. It was sharp; I could feel the edge slicing into my skin.

Without hesitation, Cassandra raised her sword. "Let her go."

Aphrodite waved a hand at him. "Let her go, Ares. Our fight isn't with her right now."

Unfortunately, I didn't think Ares was listening. To anything. It looked like he'd gone completely crazy. He pressed the blade harder against my neck. Any more and I would be in dire trouble without a healer like Chiron to mend me. "She's here to assassinate us. She's working for Hades."

"Hades is dead, darling," she said to him, trying to make him see reason.

"No, he's alive. He comes to me in my dreams." Panic and fear strangled his voice.

Apparently, Aphrodite could also hear it, because she lifted a hand toward him, to soothe him. "Let her go. We will have our revenge on her, but not today."

His hand started to shake, and I feared he would cut me when he truly didn't mean to do it.

"Let her go!" Cassandra moved so quickly I hardly registered it. The moment her hand reached Ares' head, a light came out of her palm and he was blasted backward, landing on his ass a few feet away.

I gaped at her, as did Aphrodite. "What did you do?" I asked.

Wide-eyed Cassandra glanced at her hand. "I don't know."

"Well, whatever it was. It was pretty cool." I smiled at her.

"Melany! Watch out!"

Lucian's warning reached me too late. My head whipped up just as the dragon was almost upon us, her mouth open wide. A stream of ice shot out, and I felt the chill graze my shoulder. When I turned toward Aphrodite my eyes widened.

The ice beam pierced her chest, freezing half her body.

The evil goddess fell to the ground, and I

crouched next to her, lifting her body onto my lap. Her skin was so cold, that it felt like frigid daggers puncturing my hands while I held her. I didn't know why, but remorse filled me. That woman had hurt so many people. She'd tried to kill me in more than one occasion, and still, I felt something as she lay dying in my arms.

When Aphrodite looked up at me, there were tears in her eyes. As they rolled down her cheeks they turned into shards of ice. "Follow the stars," she croaked.

"What?"

"Follow the stars to the Cave of Memory…" Her voice trailed off.

"What does that mean?" but it was too late.

She was gone.

Her eyelids slowly fluttered closed, long eyelashes freezing them shut forever.

A long, guttural moan escaped Ares as he looked down at Aphrodite's frozen body, and I almost felt bad for him. I could hear the anguish in his cry.

He took to the sky like a torpedo, his sharp spear poised in front of him. Khione swerved back toward him, but Ares didn't get out of the way. He flew right toward her. Mouth opening, she breathed ice again, hitting him on the leg but it didn't stop him.

Landing on top of the dragon's back, he thrust his spear into her side. The dragon roared as Ares pulled his weapon out and rammed it back in, over and over again, until the side of the dragon was a gory mess.

The others landed on the ground next to me while I pushed Aphrodite's body off my lap, laying her as gently as I could onto the earth—although she was beyond caring at that point. I stood beside my friends, and we watched Ares and the dragon fight to the bitter end.

With the God of War still affixed to her back, she collided into the side of a rising cliff, breaking off half the rock face. It came crashing down, hitting the dragon and Ares along the way. With one last roar, Khione crashed into the ground, the ragged boulders completely covering her and Ares' bodies.

CHAPTER EIGHTEEN

MELANY

*L*ucian glanced at me. "I sure hope Aphrodite told you what you needed to know."

"I don't know. She told me something, but I'm not sure what to make of it."

"Can we get out of here now?" Jasmine asked, shivering. The cold seemed to be seeping into our pores even more than before.

I nodded. "Yeah, let's go home." Before Cassandra could move away though, I grabbed her arm. "I don't know what you did there, but thank you for doing it."

"I thought he was going to kill you," she murmured.

"He would've but you blasted him." Taking her hand, I examined it. "I think maybe you just discovered a new power. Light power. You're a superhero now." Her unease was evident, so I let her hand go.

A few minutes later, after getting Cassandra tied to Lucian again, we flew into the sky and headed back to the chasm that led up to the gate. I thought about the ramifications of our journey here. We had inadvertently killed two more Gods, but I believed that if Ares hadn't jumped onto Khione's back, she might have tried to kill us too.

Someone didn't want me to talk to Aphrodite.

Someone didn't want me to have the information she possessed about the Cave of Memory.

It was obvious now, I'd been wrong about who wanted to resurrect Zeus, and who had been messing around with time and death. It hadn't been Aphrodite. So, if not her, then who? Who had to gain from Zeus's resurrection? The list was long. Not everyone at the academy had been happy with the outcome of the Battle of Pecunia, and definitely not with my involvement with it. Yet, in my vision, the Fates had said "her", so it had to be a woman.

That made the list a bit smaller, but not by much.

I let everyone go up before me, but before I ascended through the hole, I glanced over at the pond and rockslide that had buried Khione and Ares. I expected to see Khione's big blue scaled body covered in boulders and dirt, but all I saw was the rocks.

Considering the changes in time and in death, I wondered if maybe—like that man on the pier that I thought I had saved—Khione hadn't died. However, if the ice dragon didn't die, so maybe Ares didn't either, nor did Aphrodite. Maybe they were walking around with mortal wounds in their bodies, but still breathing.

A shudder rushed up my body at the thought, but I didn't let it stop me from flying up through the chasm, and out onto the barren field of the under-world. Once there, Lucian closed the metal gate over the hole, and using the key, I locked it. As soon as it was sealed, the ground beneath our feet started to move. The wind picked up; dirt and big chunks of the earth rolled over the entrance, covering it up, until there was no indication there was anything there at all.

I didn't know if Ares and Aphrodite had

survived, but if they had, they still weren't getting out of Tartarus. That I would make sure of.

Now that we were back on the plains, we walked back to the river's edge.

"Charon! I need your boat again!" I shouted into the ether, hoping the skeletal butler was listening, as usual.

After waiting for about five minutes, a thick fog rolled down the river, and the boat emerged from the mist with Charon at the stern, steering with his long wooden pole. The ship stopped in front of us, and the wooden plank magically appeared on shore. We boarded, and Charon sailed us back around the river to the spot where we had started.

"Thank you, Charon," I offered once we were back on land.

"I am always at your service, my lady, just as Lord Hades instructed." He inclined his head. Before long, the fog rolled up and over the ship and him, and he disappeared.

Lucian turned to me. "What does that mean?"

"It's nothing." I brushed off his question, and started walking back to the tunnel.

When he caught up with me, I knew he wasn't going to let it go.

"Doesn't sound like nothing. Sounds very much like something major."

"Charon is just being overly dramatic. It's what he does. I think he thinks he's in some Shakespearean play." I gave him a little smile, to hopefully placate him.

I didn't want to tell him that according to Charon, Hades left me the keys to the kingdom. Honestly, I didn't fully believe it myself, so the last thing I wanted to do was engage in possibly false speculations. It wouldn't do Lucian any good, or me for that matter. It was a situation that I wasn't ready to deal with yet.

"Let's get back to the academy and gather in the dining hall—I'm starving," I added, as my stomach growled. "Then we can figure out together what Aphrodite's information means, if anything."

"Yeah, I didn't get to eat my Danish," Ren mumbled.

Chuckling, Jasmine patted him on the back. "I would think after all of that, you wouldn't have an appetite."

He shrugged. "I'm pretty much hungry all the time. Nothing's really going to change that."

Once we were topside, it was night outside. We flew back to the academy, and as I'd experienced before, time had passed differently there than it had in the underworld. When we arrived at the school, everyone was asleep, so we snuck into the dining hall, hoping we could rustle up some food. Usually, there was always something in the kitchen, stashed away in the refrigerator.

During our first year, Dionysus showed us where the best stuff was kept. As usual, he was right, and we all stacked plates with pastries and fruit. Commandeering a nice-sized tub of whipped cream cheese, I dipped my fruit into it.

Food in hand, we sat at our usual table and tried to make sense of what Aphrodite had told me.

"So, she said follow the stars?" Jasmine asked.

I nodded.

"Are you sure she wasn't just babbling? She was dying."

"If she had just said follow the stars, maybe, but she repeated it and said follow the stars to find the Cave of Memory."

"Could you be talking about the Sky realm?" Lucian asked. "Thanatos was the one who directed you to Aphrodite. Maybe he was just trying to throw you off the trail. Protecting himself." He shook his head. "I find it hard to believe that death doesn't know where the Fates are. I mean, they work hand in hand."

"I know, it's just that out of all of the Gods, death, I think, is the only one who is honest."

Lucian nodded. "Yeah. You're probably right."

"Besides, I really don't want to go back there for any reason. Nyx is not a forgiving person. I could just imagine where she would snap me next, once she realizes I escaped Asphodel Meadows. I really don't want to find out." I took a strawberry, scooped a lot of cream cheese with it, and popped it into my mouth, instantly feeling better.

"Maybe we should check in the Hall of Knowledge," Lucian suggested. "It was useful to us last time."

"That's a good idea." I finished what was on my plate. "Why don't you guys head there, and I'll catch up."

"What are you going to do?" Lucian asked, his voice heavy with concern. He probably thought I was going to disappear again without a trace.

A part of me wanted to tell him that I feared the same thing.

I lifted my plate. "I'm going to get some more cream cheese. There is no way I'm squandering this opportunity to gorge."

Chuckling, he stood. "Okay, then meet us there."

Jasmine jumped to her feet. "I'm going to go check in with Mia. If what you say is true about the time, we might've been gone for days instead of just a few hours. I don't want her to think I'd left without telling her."

As everyone filed out of the dining hall to go to the Hall of Knowledge, well Jasmine went to find Mia first, I ventured back into the kitchen. Ever since I'd come back from Asphodel Meadows, I had a serious sweet tooth. All I wanted to do was eat pastries, pancakes with whipped cream, and my favorite whipped cream cheese. I supposed that seeing what Hecate had been dining on for months would do that to a person.

Using a big spoon, I scooped up some cream cheese from the tub and put it in my mouth. I nearly moaned in delight, but the sound of movement behind stopped me. I turned to see a figure in the shadows.

"What are you doing in here?" The figure stepped into the light. It was Hera, and I was really surprised to see her. When Zeus was alive, she really didn't have much to do with the running of the academy, except for teaching one class about the history of the Gods and the school, which didn't really change after his death.

"I'd ask you the same thing."

She lifted her hands, revealing a big bowl of chocolate pudding between them. "It's my one weakness."

It was the most surprising thing she could've ever showed me, and it knocked me off guard. I laughed so hard my stomach hurt.

"I didn't take you for a secret nighttime eater," I admitted.

She chuckled, then smoothed a hand over one ample hip. "I didn't come by this figure honestly."

That made me giggle even more. This was a side of the matriarch Goddess that I'd never seen before. That, I would never have even guessed. It was too bad that she didn't reveal this side of her more often, because it was really charming.

"Since you are out of bed when you shouldn't be," she added, "come with me and I'll show you something special."

"What?"

"That would ruin the surprise, now wouldn't it?"

"I'm not big on surprises, to be honest Hera."

She waved a bejeweled hand at me. "You'll like this one." She started to walk out of the kitchen.

I was feeling pretty light and breezy, with a belly full of sweetness, so I decided to follow her. What would be the harm?

As we walked the west wing corridor toward her hall, Hera gave me a side-eye look. "I've been told you were gone for a few days here and there. Where have you been running off to?"

"Nowhere special." Just because we shared a love of sweetness in the dead of night, didn't mean I trusted her with the truth.

"I know you're a great soldier, Melany, with a lot of power, but you should remember to be careful out there. It's not always safe for a girl like you."

We rounded the corner, walking toward the entrance to her hall. Something about what she'd just said bothered me, and I started to slow down my pace. Stopping, she turned to look at me.

"Is there something wrong?"

It was then that I spotted something behind her that made my heart race. There were small pinpoints of white light illuminating her hall's doors. They glowed and sparkled, looking just like stars in the night sky.

Suddenly, I remembered that the night I had

the vision about the Fates, I had sleepwalked across the academy, ending up here. In Hera's Hall. In the hall of the Goddess of the Stars.

"Follow the stars..."

Recognition slammed into me, and I knew how to get to the Cave of Memory. It was through Hera's Hall. How to get through it without alerting the Goddess, well that was a whole other problem that needed to be solved. Yet, I was just overjoyed that I figured out the mystery.

"Um, I just remembered that my friends are waiting for me."

Her head tilted to the side, carefully regarding me. "Really?"

"Yup, they are expecting me. So, you know, if I don't show up, they'll definitely raise the alarm and come looking for me."

She nodded, and smoothed a hand over her updo. "Well, then, you shouldn't keep them waiting. What I was going to show you will wait until next time."

"Great." I tipped my head to her, and turned, getting the hell out of there.

I had a feeling, a dark ominous feeling, that Hera may have been about to show me just how I was going to disappear for good.

CHAPTER NINETEEN

MELANY

J ran all the way to the Hall of Knowledge, thankful that I no longer had to break in through a secret portal in the maze, like Lucian and I did years ago. Athena had decided that the information and knowledge she'd been guarding for hundreds of years, should be available to all the Gods, demigods, and recruits at the academy. So, she had the new hall built, and all the books and scrolls relocated.

The others had books open, pouring over them when I ran in, breathing hard.

"What's wrong?" Lucian was immediately at my side.

"I figured out what 'follow the stars' means."

"You figured that out in a tub of cream cheese?" Georgina teased.

"No, when Hera discovered me in the kitchen and invited me to her hall."

Everyone looked at me funny. I didn't blame them. It was an unusual set of circumstances.

"There are stars all over the doors to her hall. She's also the Goddess of the Stars, and when I had the dream about the Fates, I woke up from it in her hall."

"Could be a coincidence," Lucian suggested.

I cocked an eyebrow. "When is anything a coincidence at the academy?"

"Good point."

"Now what?" Ren asked from his perch on one of the big, mahogany reading tables. "We go into Hera's Hall, and then? We still don't know what to look for or how it leads to the Cave of Memory."

Lucian lifted the book he'd been reading. "This is a book on the galaxies and constellations. Remember during first year in Hera's lecture hall? The dome ceiling was a map of the sky with all the constellations."

When he set the book down, opening it to the page he'd been perusing, I stepped up to him.

"Maybe one of the constellations will lead us to a portal, a door, or a gate."

I smiled at him. "Look at you, being a smarty-pants."

Chuckling, he swung an arm around my shoulders, and pulled me into him. "I guess I'm not just a pretty face."

"Ha! I wouldn't go that far."

Leaning in, he brushed his lips against mine. It was the first time since I got back from the meadows that he'd tried to kiss me. I let it happen, even though I felt awkward about it, and I hated that I did. Something had fundamentally shifted between us, but I wasn't exactly sure what it was.

When Lucian pulled back, he had a similar look in his eyes. He seemed as confused as I was about what had just happened. Something occurred when our two timelines merged, and it was more than just about his and the others' powers.

Jasmine and Mia came into the library holding hands. "So, what did we miss?"

"Melany figured out that we need to be in Hera's Hall to find the way to the Cave of Memory, and Lucian thinks there might be something we can use in that boring book on constellations," Ren stated.

"Cool." Jasmine nodded.

Mia looked over at me. "I'm glad to see you back, Mel."

"I'm glad to be back."

"Libra," Cassandra blurted out of the blue, and we all turned to look at her.

"What about Libra?" I asked.

"I'm a Libra," Mia stated, matter-of-factly.

"Libra's constellation actually belongs to Astraea, who was the Goddess of Justice," "Libra is shown holding a set of scales, but those scales belong to Astraea. She was rumored to have been the last immortal to have lived on Earth among the humans. Eventually, she left, due to her disgust of humanity's wickedness and brutality."

"Okay, but what does that have to do with finding the Cave of Memory?" I asked.

"Astraea was also known as the Star Goddess." Cassandra turned the book and pushed it toward me.

Glancing down at the page she'd turned to, I found there was a picture of the Goddess, and the constellation connected to her. It was a triangle with two lines coming down from it. It represented the scales of justice. "I remember seeing this on the ceiling of Hera's lecture hall."

With my words, everyone came over and crowded around the book to have a look.

Jasmine nodded. "Me too. It's on the upper left side. One of the lines coming down points to the floor."

I smiled at Cassandra. "How do you know about constellations?"

"They are very much connected to prophecy," she confessed. "Apollo has been teaching me."

"Okay, so we have the pieces, now how do we use them?" Georgina asked.

My shoulders lifted and fell. "I guess we've got to sneak into Hera's Hall."

"Oh, is that all?" Jasmine snorted.

"Hey, we just went to Tartarus and back. This should be a piece of cake."

It wasn't a piece of cake. In fact, it was pretty damn hard.

Firstly, we decided not to do it that night, as we were all exhausted. I ended up sleeping over twelve hours, and Georgina had to wake me up by dribbling some cold water onto my face. Afterward, we all had classes we needed to attend. I, in particular, had been very negligent with my academy duties, so much so, that Prometheus called me to his office to have a chat.

At first, I thought he was going to scold me for the fact that we stole the key to Tartarus, and had gone down there. Yet, someone had the presence of mind to return the key when we got back. I wasn't sure who it had been, no one informed me, but when I walked out onto the platform of the highest tower, the key was there, back on Prometheus's belt.

"I understand that the past couple of years have been difficult for you, Melany," Prometheus stated. "You lost your mother and your home. You were treated unfairly by the previous administration, and you lost a... mentor in the big battle."

He was choosing his words carefully, I noticed. The true sign of a diplomat.

"And I feel like we have given you a lot of leeway because of this, but you have responsibilities here at the academy now. You have proven yourself to be a powerful soldier and a competent leader, so now it's time to pass on that knowledge, training the next generation of soldiers."

I nodded. "You've been more than lenient with me. And I appreciate that, Prometheus." Then, I decided to just throw caution to the wind. "But I have a question for you."

Intrigued, he inclined his head for me to continue.

"Haven't you noticed that something is going on?"

"What do you mean?"

"Well, I'm sure Hephaistos has told you about the list of recruits for the shadowboxes, or I should say, the lack of a list."

"He did mention it, yes."

"Don't you think that's weird?"

He shrugged. "Not really. It turned out to be a clerical error."

"A clerical error?" I gave him a look.

"Yes."

"So, Hephaistos has a new list?"

"Not that it is any of your concern, but yes, he has a proper list of candidates to send shadowboxes to this year."

A deep frown crinkled my brows. I wasn't sure what to make of that. I would definitely check with Hephaistos, which I was sure Prometheus would know. Was he lying to me? Did he know what was going on? Or was he as much in the dark as the rest of us?

"Is there something else you're not saying, Melany? You seemed very adamant about telling me about that list. As if that proved a theory of yours."

Should I tell him about death? Should I tell him about my trip to Asphodel Meadows, and about the vision Cassandra sent me about the Fates? Prometheus wasn't at all like Zeus, but I still wasn't one hundred percent sure I could trust him with what I knew.

Sighing, I shook my head. "No, I just thought you should know about the list. I found it very odd." I got up from the chair. "Thank you for the pep talk. I won't let you down, sir."

"See that you don't. Others here at the academy do not share my charity toward you, and I do not wish to prove them right."

I gave him a little salute. "From now on, I'll be the model soldier of the Gods' Army." Of course, I was lying through my teeth, and I suspected he knew that and was just giving lip service for those at the academy who had been complaining about me.

Once he nodded, I left, leaping off the platform and flying down to the bottom floor of Zeus's Hall. I had no intention of being a model anything, but I decided I better put in some effort to throw everyone off my track. Tonight, if everything went well, my friends and I would be heading to the Cave of Memory to fix time and death, since no one else seemed to give a damn about it.

After I left his office, I spent some time training at the elemental dome. Thankfully, I only had a few recruits to teach about lightning. Then it was dinner time, and we all met in the dining hall as we normally did. We ate, and planned. Tonight, we would pack up some supplies, I had no idea what we were going to need, but rope and the like sounded like a good idea. I told everyone to meet me in the maze, and I would use the shadows to get into Hera's Hall.

That had not gone to plan.

When I took everyone through the shadows, we ended up everywhere but inside Hera's Hall. One time, we ended up walking in on Dionysus and Demeter getting high on the weed that Demeter grew in Dionysus's laboratory. Thankfully, they didn't make a big deal out of it, and just told us to be more careful about where we traveled.

On the last try, we appeared just outside of the closed doors of Hera's hall.

"Okay, so now what?" Jasmine asked.

"Break in." I grabbed the big brass door handle and tried to turn it. Of course, the door was locked.

"Maybe we should abort." Ren looked back

down the hall nervously. "I really don't want to get caught. Hera seems like she's this matronly woman, but she scares me. I don't think anyone can be a loving, reasonable, compassionate person and have been married to Zeus."

We all agreed. I still remembered the glee on her face when I was being tortured with lightning, after I'd been caught leaving the academy during our first year. And when Hades showed up to claim me as his apprentice, she'd been one of the first ones to call for the guards to arrest him, or worse.

Hera was not a woman we wanted to piss off, but I had to get into her hall and find the entrance to the Cave of Memory.

I tried the door again, but I couldn't even rattle it. Then, I produced flames and tried to melt the doorknob. That didn't work. I knew lightning wouldn't help, and neither would water. We needed something stronger to break the lock.

Glancing over at Georgina, I gave her my sauciest grin. "Want to test out your new metal hand?"

"Not really," she replied.

"C'mon. It'll be cool."

She shook her head but stepped up in front of the door. "I think you really got this made for yourself." Her metal fingers wrapped around the brass handle, and she squeezed.

At first, I didn't think it was going to give, but Georgina put all her energy into it, and was gifted with the sound of the brass compressing into a tiny little ball. When she pulled the handle off, I reached in the hole, finessed the lock open with nimble fingers, and pushed the doors open.

CHAPTER TWENTY

MELANY

*W*hen we entered the hall, I half expected to see Hera standing there, waiting for us with a dagger in one hand and a tub of chocolate pudding in the other. Yet, as it was, the hall was dark and empty. We moved quickly into Hera's lecture room with the domed ceiling full of stars. Someone flicked on the lights, and we searched the sky for the Libra constellation.

"It's not here," Cassandra whispered.

"It has to be," I pressed.

She pointed to the area on the dome where I

remembered seeing it. "It should be there, but it isn't."

"Shit!" My hand smacked the wall in frustration. "Why can't just one thing be easy?"

Frowning, Lucian looked up at the ceiling. "Do that again."

"What?"

"Hitting the wall. When you did that, the stars moved. There are new constellations now."

"Are you sure?"

"Do it again, and watch."

I smacked the wall, feeling the impact of it resonate up my arm. He was right, there was a shift in the stars. They moved around to form different shapes. I must've been hitting some kind of controls along the wall.

Forming a ball of fire in my hand, I inspected the surface. It took a few minutes, but I finally spotted a control panel of sorts. It was like playing with a temperature switch—not too hot, not too cold, just right in the middle. Trying to find that right spot though, the middle, proved difficult.

I moved the gauges back and forth, hence moving the stars on the sky dome back and forth, and round and around. Sometimes I would get one or two in the right position, but then I couldn't get the next ones in the right spot, without upsetting the balance of the original constellations.

"Agh! I'm going to break this piece of shit in about two minutes if it doesn't work."

"You need to be patient," Georgina reminded.

I gave her a look. "When have you ever known me to be patient?"

"K, guys, I really don't want to get caught in here," Ren urged. "Let's either figure it out, or get the hell out."

Cassandra approached me. "Can I try?"

Shrugging, I gestured to the wall. "Knock yourself out."

I watched as she set her hand over the mechanism, shut her eyes, and made it move. We all looked up at the dome as the lights quickly shuffled around, lining up in complicated patterns. Suddenly, along the far right three stars formed a triangle, and two others drew down, forming two legs, while the last one settled in at the tip of the closest leg. It was the Libra constellation.

"Damn girl, you did it." I laughed as I walked over to the far right side of the room.

"Now what?" Jasmine asked, looking around us. "Did anyone see a door open, or a portal?"

Hovering in the air, I lifted my hand and

dragged it over the longest leg of the constellation. When I reached the very last star, I felt something under my fingertips. "There's something here."

"What?"

Instead of answering, I pressed my fingers down on the raised dot on the ceiling. There was a loud clicking noise, then a whirring.

"What did you do Mel?" Jasmine demanded.

"I, ah, kind of pushed a button, I think."

The next second, the whole room began to spin.

It was like being in the Graviton carnival ride. The pressure from the spinning pushed us up against the wall. I couldn't even lift an arm as my body was forced into the side of the space. Glancing across, I saw Lucian tilted sideways along the wall. The centrifugal force defying the laws of gravity as the room rotated at an incredible speed.

After an undetermined amount of time, I could feel the rotation slowing, until my feet touched the ground again. Then, it stopped, as if someone had stepped on the brakes, making the items and people who had been pressed into the walls crash to the floor, including Lucian.

Dizzy, I looked up at the ceiling, to see the Libra constellation on the other side of the dome, the end of its leg pointing right to the door. It was as good as an exit sign to me, as I'd ever seen.

"What just happened?" Ren asked, rubbing his head. He was probably sporting a headache, because I sure was.

"I'm pretty certain we just traveled somewhere else." Georgina made her way across the room to the door.

"Remind me never to go anywhere with you guys again." Doubling over, Mia vomited.

Going to her side, Jasmine swept a hand over her back. "You'll get used to it."

Wiping her mouth with the back of her hand, Mia straightened. "I don't think I want to, to be honest."

We all gathered at the door. Anticipation made my hand shake as I grabbed the handle, turned it, and pushed open the door. Again, I half-expected to see Hera standing there with a big grin, yelling "Surprise!" But Hera wasn't there, no one was. In fact, nothing was. Or at least, at first glance, that's what it looked like. Nothing.

A straight, vast, sand-covered land stretched out before us as far as the eye could see—in every direction. It looked like the desert but without any dunes, valleys, or oasis to be found. Just a flat, desolate, sweep of land.

"Where are we?" Lucian set a hand on my shoulder.

I shook my head. "I don't know."

"It looks like nothing." Cassandra's voice was as flat as what spanned in front of us.

"Maybe that's what it is," I suggested, "the nothingness before life happens."

"Where's this cave?" Ren took the first step out onto the sandy plain, and I stepped out next to him.

"It has to be here somewhere." Unfurling my wings, I lifted my hand into the air. "There's no breeze whatsoever, so flying should be pretty easy."

It wasn't long before we were all airborne— Cassandra was attached to Lucian again. Even at the height we flew, there was still the expanse of flat land that stretched out until the horizon. If I didn't know any better, I would've said the Earth was as flat as a pancake.

We flew for what seemed like hours before we had to land to share the water canteens, and then we went back up to fly some more. As I looked out over the ground, I tried to keep my gaze to the distance. There had to be something there.

After another hour, Jasmine suggested we return

to the room and go back to the academy. "There is nothing here, Mel. We're going to get lost and die here if we don't go back."

Fear exuded from her every word, and I didn't blame her for it. I was afraid too of the same thing. However, I was also afraid of time being erased and death going on holiday, not to mention, of someone trying to resurrect Zeus.

"You guys go back. I'm going to go a little further."

"Wait," Lucian pointed to the horizon. "There's something there."

Squinting, I peered into the distance and saw a dark shape rising. "It's a mountain."

It was. One tall mountain in the middle of nothing. And carved into the side of that mountain was a cave.

We had found it.

One by one, we landed on the narrow edge before the cave. Lucian untied Cassandra while Jasmine lit a fire ball, so did I, and we went inside. It looked exactly like the dug out, rocky tunnel from my vision. The deeper we went in, the cooler and damper it got, until fog started to ripple on the stone floor.

"This is it," I assured. "I saw this place."

"So did I," Cassandra affirmed.

We kept going, the tunnel getting narrower, so we had to go single file. I led the group with Cassandra behind me, Lucian, Georgina, Jasmine and Mia following her, and Ren as the last one. The mist along the rocky floor thickened and crawled up the sides of the tunnel, and then swirled overhead. After a time, it became disorienting since everything around us looked the same.

After a few more steps, I started to question whether I was even walking on the ground, or sideways along the wall. I quickly glanced behind me to see where Cassandra was, but I didn't see her directly. All I saw was strands of her red hair hanging down from the ceiling. I looked back further through the fog and saw the bobbing of Jasmine's fire ball along the floor, or what I perceived was the floor.

The laws of physics didn't seem to exist in here. That was where the Fates lived and did as they pleased.

Going a bit farther, the tunnel led us into a cavern. It was there that the fog lifted, revealing that we'd all been walking on different surfaces, in different directions. I was upside down, Cassandra was sideways and to my right, Lucian was on the ground, Ren and Jasmine were at an angle, so was Mia, but on the opposite side. Georgina was also upside down, yet, somehow, she had ended up in front of me.

"Well, this is a bit unsettling," Georgina mumbled.

"I think if we all just walk along the walls we will end up on the floor with Lucian," I instructed.

Everyone did as I said, and we all came together in a huddle on the ground—or what we all assumed was the ground. Once there, together, we assessed our situation.

The image was straight from my vision of the Fates, except the three cloaked sisters weren't present. All that was left was their spinning wheel, a ball of golden line on the ground, beside the stool I'd seen Clotho sitting in as she spun the threads of life.

Beyond that, hanging from every possible spot on the cavern ceiling, were varying lengths of golden thread. They were the life lines of every mortal, and God, who had ever existed.

"Holy crap," Lucian muttered. "Are those…?"

I nodded. "Yup, those are threads of life."

Everyone gaped in amazement.

Ren stepped forward and trailed his fingers over

the ends of a few of the shorter lines. "Where it's cut, is when they died?"

"Yes," I confirmed, trying hard not to feel too awestruck.

"Where are the Fates?" Jasmine moved around, trying to make sense of the place, as if there were other rooms where the sisters could be hiding.

There weren't. That was it. One big empty cavern.

We'd come all this way, gone through hell, for nothing. Disappointment flooded me so quickly that I felt dizzy. I reached out a hand toward the stone wall to steady myself.

"This is kind of cool." I looked over to see Ren walking up one side of the cavern, to take a closer peek at some of the threads hanging there. "If you look real close, you can see names on them."

"Really?" Wide-eyed, Jasmine peered around at all the lines. "You mean we could find our own threads and see how long we'll live?"

"Yes, you could, but would you want to?" Georgina ran her fingers over the spinning wheel. It moved a little, and she snatched back her hand.

"I don't know," Jasmine mumbled, "maybe." Her attention went to Mia, who was still looking a bit unsteady, leaning against one of the rock walls. "Mia, would you want know?"

Her girlfriend swallowed and shook her head. "No way. That feels way too creepy."

Meanwhile, my head was spinning. Licking my lips, I tried to keep the contents of my stomach down. I couldn't believe we'd come all this way to find no answers. Where did the Fates go? And how was I going to find them now?

"Oh, damn."

I turned to see Ren nearby, peering into his hand where he held a severed piece of golden line.

"I found Revana's thread."

Biting down on my bottom lip, I turned away from him and the evidence of my mistake. I closed my eyes for a moment, trying to calm my body. My guts were roiling, and I wasn't sure I wasn't going to get sick.

"Should we look for Zeus's thread?" Lucian asked. "If we took it, then no one could resurrect him."

Everyone split up, starting to search through the threads on the stone floor.

Slowly, I leaned over, putting my hands on my thighs and took in some deep breaths. It was then that my gaze caught something on the ground, near my boot. It was a severed golden thread, but there was something different about that line. The color was darker, more bronze than gold, like a burnt piece of wheat.

Reaching down, I picked it up. The second it was in my hand, I knew who it belonged to. I didn't even have to read the name spun into the side. I could feel the power vibrating against my skin, like electricity, like a dark storm brewing. Even now. Even severed, I could feel *him*.

My heart leapt in pure joy.

"Mel? Did you find something?"

I jolted at the question, and quickly slid the golden thread into my pants' pocket. Lucian stared at me, waiting for an answer.

"No, nothing."

As everyone went back to their search of the threads on the floor, I slowly rubbed my hand over my pocket, and smiled.

Thank you for reading Demigods Academy 5.
Don't miss FINAL book!
We hope you enjoyed Melany's adventures and can't wait to share more with you. In the meantime,

we would love to read your opinion on Amazon and Goodreads. Please consider leaving a review for us. **We'd love it.**

And if you don't want to miss our future books, you just need to join our lists of readers below.

Sign Up to get our EMAILS at:
www.KieraLegend.com
www.ElisaSAmore.com/Vip-List

Sign Up to get our SMS (US only):
Text AMORE to 77948
Text LEGEND to 77948

ABOUT THE AUTHOR

Elisa S. Amore is the number-one bestselling author of the paranormal romance saga *Touched*.

Vanity Fair Italy called her "the undisputed queen of romantic fantasy." After the success of Touched, she produced the audio version of the saga featuring Hollywood star Matt Lanter (*90210, Timeless, Star Wars*) and Disney actress Emma Galvin, narrator of *Twilight* and *Divergent*. Elisa is now a full-time writer of young adult fantasy. She's wild about pizza and also loves traveling, which she calls a source of constant inspiration. With her successful series about life and death, Heaven and Hell, she has built a loyal fanbase on social media that continues to grow, and has quickly become a favorite author for thousands of readers in the U.S.

Visit Elisa S. Amore's website and join her List of Readers at www.ElisaSAmore.com and Text AMORE to 77948 for new release alerts.

FOLLOW ELISA S. AMORE:

facebook.com/eli.amore
instagram.com/eli.amore
twitter.com/ElisaSAmore
elisa.amore@touchedsaga.com

***

Kiera Legend writes Urban Fantasy and Paranormal Romance stories that bite. She loves books, movies and Tv-Shows. Her best friends are usually vampires, witches, werewolves and angels. She never hangs out without her little dragon. She especially likes writing kick-ass heroines and strong world-buildings and is excited for all the books that are coming!

Text LEGEND to 77948 to don't miss any of them (US only) or sign up at www.kieralegend.com to get an email alert when her next book is out.

FOLLOW KIERA LEGEND:

facebook.com/groups/kieralegend
facebook.com/kieralegend
authorkieralegend@gmail.com